THE
DEADLY
NEWS

JON HORNER

PublishAmerica
Baltimore

Softcover 9781413725322
PUBLISHED BY PUBLISHAMERICA, LLLP
www.publishamerica.com
Baltimore

Printed in the United States of America

To Darla, Chase, Madison, my parents, Bill and Adella Horner; and the memory of my beloved Aunt Irene for the encouragement to continue with my writing. A special thank you to Donna Richards. Thanks so much for reviewing my manuscript and finding my numerous errors. The time you spent on the book was invaluable.

CHAPTER 1

THE news of Haley Fulz tragic death swept through the quaint town of Bouvier, Missouri, and much of surrounding Barry County in a swift fashion. In communities of this nature, when a beautiful and popular teenager dies in an inexplicable car wreck it doesn't take much time for the horrible news to make the rounds. But this wasn't the death of just any seventeen year old girl. This was the death of Haley Fulz.

Haley Fulz was a high school senior, captain of the Bouvier High volleyball team, and a very talented vocalist in the Bouvier all-girls choir. She was also the girl friend of Chad McMasters, a freshman journalism major at the University of Missouri in Columbia. Chad was the son of Mitch and Clare McMasters, third generation owners of the venerable *Bouvier Gazette*, the county's oldest and most prominent newspaper. In light of his family's historic status in the county, he was viewed as being quite the catch for Haley Fulz.

Haley Fulz grew up most of her life in the town of Bouvier, Missouri, located in Barry County in the midst of the beautiful Ozarks hills in Southwest Missouri. Her father, Jake Fulz, ran a delivery route for a regional uniform supply company that supplied uniforms for local auto repair businesses. Jake Fulz split from the Fulz family confines on a snowy winter night at least ten years earlier. He had maintained little contact after he had abandoned his family. Her mom, Jackie Fulz, had worked at a local electronics components manufacturer doing assembly work for over fifteen years. When she was younger, Jackie had been quite the beauty. However, the stress and grind of the factory life and being the sole provider for her and Haley had taken its toll. The result of her daily pressures had become clearly visible on her once beautiful features.

Even though she had clearly not grown up as a child of privilege, Haley Fulz had been able to maintain friendships with classmates from all kinds of economic and social backgrounds in Bouvier. Her physical beauty, long blond hair, and beautiful green eyes had certainly opened up a lot of doors. But she also had an intellect and a warm, engaging personality that enabled her to maintain connections that would have quickly burned out if she had been just another dizzy blond beauty. Haley Fulz certainly had a bright future ahead of her until the car she was driving went off the dreadful road at the top of Roaring River State Park in Barry County.

The Barry County Sheriff, Buford Blakeley, had estimated that Haley's car, a new Honda S2000 Roadster convertible, had been traveling at a high rate of speed when it apparently failed to make the curve at the hill overlooking the beautiful Roaring River State Park. The wreck took place at approximately 11:00 pm on a Tuesday evening in early September. After her roadster left the road, it had flown off the steep embankment and finally touched the earth approximately 100 to 150 feet below the highway. The horrific nature of the crash led Sheriff Blakeley to estimate that Haley died on impact.

The Honda Roadster convertible had been an early high school graduation gift from the McMasters family. Haley had received it from Chad's family earlier that summer. When Haley was presented with the car, it caused an unbelievable stir in Bouvier. No one in Bouvier could ever remember a high school romance leading to a gift of this nature. Most Bouvier

High School romances led to the receipt of a class ring, a letterman's jacket, a bad case of herpes, or an unplanned pregnancy. However, until this bequest, none had led to a shiny new red roadster. The receipt of a $30,000 vehicle from her boyfriend's family had certainly caused a considerable amount of jealously and ill will from her classmates. Now it would only serve as a cruel reminder of a young romance that held so much promise.

Many in town felt that the gift said more about the arrogance of the McMasters family and their consistent desire to flaunt their supposed wealth than about the seriousness of the romance between Haley Fulz and Chad McMasters. The existence of a persistent rumor going around town that there was a $30,000 lien against Haley's "gift" added fuel to the belief that the McMasters were long on pride and a little short on cash.

An autopsy would be performed, but most knew that the report would confirm the only consolation available to her friends and family, that Haley didn't suffer in her death. Her death was instantaneous at the moment of impact. In the wee hours after her death, Jackie Fulz wrestled with the decision of whether or not to have an autopsy performed. She finally decided on the autopsy. Jackie reasoned that she didn't want anyone going around saying that Haley had been drinking or doing something bad that evening. She also figured that it would be needed for insurance purposes. She was confident that her little girl had either fallen asleep or had been distracted by a cell phone call or something of that nature and, as a result, had failed to make the tragic curve that evening.

Jackie Fulz had unanswered questions in her mind about why Haley was traveling alone and going toward the river, which was almost fifteen miles from home, at 11 p.m. on a school night. The only plausible reason to be going that direction could be that Haley was coming home from the McMasters' river cabin, which was located near the state park. But since Chad was away in Italy working on his college foreign language studies, it wouldn't make any sense for Haley to be at the cabin that evening. After several hours that fateful evening, Jackie finally resolved that her questions would never be answered and that she would be better off focusing on the wonderful aspects of her beautiful daughter's life. But deep down she knew that she would never get over the question of why Haley had been alone and near the river when she died.

CHAPTER 2

MITCH McMASTERS' family had ruled over Bouvier, Missouri, and most of Barry County for almost one hundred years through their command and ownership of the county's most prominent newspaper, the *Bouvier Gazette*. The McMasters family had possessed many flamboyant characters, and Mitch was not about to break family tradition in this area. As the third generation to guide the newspaper, he was motivated by both fear and arrogance.

The fear came from the strong family pressure and pride to continue the family legacy in the face of inherent mounting financial pressures on small town newspapers all around the nation. Although he would never admit it publicly, Mitch McMasters feared being able to continue the family legacy. Every year he could see the numbers of small town newspapers continuing to decline as more and more people obtained their news from other sources. However, he was fortunate to operate in an area of the nation which prided itself on having its local news. A local newspaper was invaluable in its ability to support the community schools and sports teams and broadcasting the academic achievements of the young men and women in the small towns covered by the local daily. The McMasters family had masterfully cultured an allegiance to their paper in each of the small towns in Barry County. If there was a sporting event, the *Bouvier Gazette* would have it covered. The school honor rolls were covered in the *Gazette* in a manner that proclaimed to the world that little Johnny or little Suzie was the smartest kid to set foot on this planet and was destined to become a rocket scientist. It was easy to see why every Bouvier resident and most of Barry County eagerly awaited the arrival of the *Bouvier Gazette*.

The McMasters family had tremendous pride in their ancestral enterprise. As the newspaper was handed down from one generation to another, the pride became stronger and stronger until in the case of Mitch McMasters, it had developed into full throttled arrogance. Mitch clearly understood the importance of his paper to the residents of Bouvier and most of Barry County. Over time Mitch began to equate the paper's importance with his own personal importance. Because of this, he loved to use the paper as his sounding board on various topics of concern in Bouvier and the surrounding small communities. He was also not shy about using his editorials to brow beat companies, businesses, or utilities into buying more advertising in his paper. It was almost comical to long-time locals to witness Mitch in action. One notable example was his editorial browbeating of a local cable TV franchise over their poor service to the surrounding communities. The locals noticed the pattern in Mitch's approval of the cable provider rose in concert with the increase in the cable company's advertising in the *Gazette*. Most observed that the cable TV company was still providing horrible service, but Mitch turned a blind eye once he editorially blackmailed them out of some precious advertising dollars.

Mitch McMasters greatly understood that his business operated in what was commonly known as the Bible belt. He also appreciated the level of power that was possessed by the church-going crowd in each of the communities his paper served. Because of this Mitch loved to proclaim, in his characteristic self righteous way, his support for every conservative cause that would come before Bouvier and the surrounding area. If you were to read his editorials, you would have to assume that Mitch McMasters was a devout Christian, the most faithful husband Barry County had ever seen, and the most trusted friend you could ever want to have. Those who truly knew the real Mitch McMasters understood that his editorials represented a fictionalized version of the man. They were consistently amazed by his smooth gall in selling his persona through his paper to the local communities. They also knew that even though many in Bouvier had become keenly aware of the real Mitch McMasters, they also knew that every time the *Bouvier Gazette* proclaimed the achievements of their child, grandchild, nephew, or cousin those people couldn't care less that Mitch was a first class hypocrite. They loved him because his paper had treated their loved one with great adulation and respect. That amazing ability to sway the public was what drove his friends and enemies crazy. For many, it was simply envy. They knew his true ways and that they were not pure. But deep down many in Bouvier secretly wished they could be just like Mitch McMasters.

Clare McMasters had grown up in Wichita, Kansas, as an only and surprisingly regular, well rounded child. Her father, Chip Blalock, worked as a mid-level executive for one of the numerous airplane manufacturers in the Wichita area. Clare's mother, Alicia Blalock, had been a noted journalism teacher in the Wichita public school system. Several of her students had gone on to journalism careers as a result of her teaching, encouragement, and passion for the field.

Like many upper middle class families in the Wichita area, the Blalocks made the lake hamlet of Castle Rock, Missouri their summer get away home. Castle Rock located on the beautiful Table Rock Lake was less than fifteen miles from Bouvier. It was during one of the family's visits to their lake home that Clare's gorgeous blue eyes and tall blonde figure caught the eye of Mitch McMasters. From that chance meeting began Clare's love affair and passion for the three things that would become the dearest to her life: Mitch McMasters, small town journalism, and the town of Bouvier, Missouri.

Clare was immediately smitten by the handsome, supremely confident, and conveniently charming Mitch McMasters. Mitch's perceived family wealth and obviously power and influence were appealing. But Clare was equally drawn to the quaint town of Bouvier, Missouri, and the ideal of the journalistic influence of the *Bouvier Gazette*. The equal draws of Mitch McMasters and the newspaper led Clare to the University of Missouri and the school's respected journalism school, otherwise known as the J-School. Her mom's background as a journalism teacher had made a profound impact on Clare's curiosity with a career in journalism. Meeting Mitch McMasters cemented her desire to venture into the field.

Clare and Mitch experienced a passionate and stormy courtship while going to school at MU. From the start it became clear to Clare that her desire to soak up all of the knowledge and expertise in journalism building was leaps and bounds greater than Mitch's. In fact, over time she began to resent the fact that a disinterested student like Mitch was taking up one of the highly coveted seats in the journalism school. How Mitch maintained his eligible seat in the J-School was a mystery to Clare and her J-School friends. Mitch would occasionally and arrogantly boast that his family knew most of the Missouri State Senate on a first name basis. This perceived influence led many J-School students to correctly conclude that Mitch McMasters was taking up precious space in the coveted journalism school because of his family's political connections. This, combined with the fact that he did not possess any journalistic or academic prowless and lacked a desire to be a true journalist, led to considerable resentment by Clare and many of her journalistic friends. Despite this level of resentment toward his seriousness toward his journalistic pursuits, Clare maintained her desire to be with Mitch. Even the widely held suspicions that he was sleeping around with other women at the university did not sway Clare from the ideal of running the *Bouvier Gazette* and being the wife of the dashing Mitch McMasters. Clare Blalock and Mitch McMasters married in the summer following their graduations from the University of Missouri in a beautiful and traditional ceremony in Clare's church in Wichita. After a honeymoon to Cancun, they settled in to run the *Bouvier Gazette*.

Mitch's family gladly turned the paper operation over to the young McMasters within a year of their arrival at the *Gazette*. Mitch's father, Winfield McMasters, was more than happy to walk away from the newspaper. Over time the small town feuds and skirmishes had quietly taken their toll on the elder McMasters. Being able to leave the paper allowed Winfield McMasters to devote more time to his true passions: sour mash whisky and Democrat politics. The continual decline of the Democrat party in Barry County and Winfield's drinking eventually got the best of him, and he died within three years after leaving the helm of the *Bouvier Gazette*.

The personal and professional partnership between Mitch and Clare McMasters had long been a stormy and equally successful merging of their talents and desires. Early on it was established that Clare would run the news gathering and reporting arm of the paper. Mitch dove full-time into editorializing on a weekly basis and gathering those precious advertising dollars. This gave Mitch the luxury of an open work schedule and an open slate to pontificate, as he loved to say, on a weekly basis on the topics of importance to Bouvier and Barry County. Or as many of the locals liked to snicker, the topics that were of importance to Mitch McMasters. Even with their roles clearly established, it still did not squelch disputes between the two over the content of the news and the tone of Mitch's legendary editorials. If there was one thing that irked Clare more than anything, it was the natural writing styling that Mitch possessed. His styling, word choice, and ability to drive home his key editorial points were very impressive, especially considering the amount of effort he put into his typical column. Quietly to herself, Clare wished she could communicate in as clear a manner as Mitch. Even with the daily tension in the air between Mitch and Clare, the *Bouvier Gazette* grew and prospered under their leadership.

Clare won over Mitch's family in her early days at the *Bouvier Gazette*. Despite moving into old offices that many young graduates of journalism school would have considered to be dated and beneath their status as journalist, Clare embraced her surroundings. Mitch wanted to remodel the newspaper headquarters in a style that befitted Mitch McMasters, but Clare insisted on keeping the historic newsroom in tact. The newspaper building had been constructed in the early 1900s, and had the look of an old newspaper right out of a Frank Capra movie. The dark woodwork had the mark of classic historic building of the early 1900s era. It may have been an old building, but it most certainly remained the best constructed structure in downtown Bouvier. Clare's desk had been used by nearly every member of the McMasters family. She continued to use the old style wooden executive office chair that had been at the desk for over forty years. To Clare the chair spoke volumes about historical strength and continuity of a prized Bouvier tradition, the *Bouvier Gazette*.

The McMasters family loved Clare's desire to embrace their historic status in the community. They knew that many strong willed young women would prefer to run away from such an intimidating heritage and declare their own new realm or era in the Bouvier community. But Clare clearly knew and treasured the value in the *Bouvier Gazette*. She was also drawn to the romantic allure of recording and reporting the history of a proud community that still had the refreshing resemblance of small towns made popular in modern television or motion pictures, such as Mayberry and Niceville. Except Bouvier wasn't a fantasy. It really did exist in Southwest Missouri, and Clare McMasters wanted to soak up every ounce of the quaint little town and its charming residents.

After the birth of their only child, Chad, Mitch began to devote more time away from the paper. His beloved pastimes had always been the lake and hanging out at the Bouvier Golf Club. Although he never developed noticeable skills at water skiing or golf, Mitch loved to regale his buddies with his latest supposed achievements on the water or at the golf links. He did however; develop an impressive track record in investments in speculative real estate. Through a series of real estate transactions, Mitch appeared to have mastered the ability to buy property rather cheaply and then turn around and sell the same property at a considerably higher price. Many locals questioned how the real estate development company, covertly owned by Mitch, could be so right so often. On many occasions Mitch purchased dilapidated properties, that would later become the prospective route of a new street, highway, or the site of a new county courthouse or jail expansion.

Mitch McMasters had formed a real estate development company with a bizarre name to hide his involvement in the questionable land deals. After a few years, some gossipy minds in the Barry County Courthouse, most notably Mary Bledsoe a clerk in the Recorder of Deeds office, quietly leaked out the news of Mitch's ownership in the covert enterprise. Being subjected to some of his own tactics did not sit well with Mitch. He vowed to himself to find out the name of the offending party. Over time he was successful, and in short order he conveniently printed an embarrassing DWI arrest involving a member of the Bledsoe family. Such was the charmed life of Mitch McMasters.

On the morning after Haley Fulz's death Clare McMasters was the first to arrive at the *Bouvier Gazette*. Dressed in her usual graceful, understated manner, Clare McMasters remained a beautiful and subtlely sexy figure at the age of forty-five.

The news of Haley's death had hit her from so many fronts. She was first and foremost trying to hold up in her deep grief for a beautiful, young girl that she had envisioned someday being a member of their family. Additionally, she had to deliver the horrible news to her son that his long-time girlfriend, the love of his young life, had died so tragically. The fact that Chad was in Italy for his college foreign language studies made it even more distressful. Clare simply wished that she could wrap her arms around Chad and let him bear his grief on her shoulder. She knew that it would benefit not only Chad but herself as well. Clare was also mourning Haley in the sense that she had been a valued employee of the newspaper during the previous two summers. With Chad being away in Italy, she and Haley had become especially close.

CHAPTER 3

THE RELATIONSHIP between Haley and Clare wasn't the only bond that had intensified when Chad left for Italy. The affair between Haley Fulz and Mitch McMasters started innocently on a late night run to deliver some newspapers to a lake side grocery store. Mitch had consumed more than a couple of Budweisers. The liquor, combined with the sight of Haley's gorgeous long legs, proved too much for his already shallow supply of personal integrity and self control. Surprisingly, Haley welcomed his overtures. Two nights later they consummated their initial flirtations at the McMaster's lake cabin. The torrid affair continued non stop during the summer until shortly before the night of Haley's death. Mitch had certainly taken part in several extramarital affairs, but he had never stooped to the level of having sex with someone young enough to be his daughter, or daughter-in-law in this situation.

Though he was quite experienced in the field of infidelity, Mitch handled this affair in a completely different way than he had the other lapses in his marital vows. Mitch's feelings for Haley were deeper than he had ever been able to conjure up in previous affairs. He became consumed with Haley. In fact, he ached to see, feel, and touch her. Each day he would eagerly finish his various business tasks and then head straight to the family's lake cabin, where he would eagerly meet Haley for their nightly rendezvous. To keep their affair from being discovered, they put together a deliberate plan to hide their liaisons. The wooded location of the lake cabin greatly assisted their desire for privacy. They also took other steps to hide their carnal ambitions. The primary o.k. signal was the placement of Mitch's car. Though it was rare, if Clare were to decide to accompany Mitch on a drive to the lake, he would park the vehicle predominately in the driveway. Otherwise, he would always park on one side of the lake cabin garage. Haley would use the other side of the garage to hide her car.

Even though they did not bring it up in their conversations together, Chad figured greatly in each of their minds and consciences in the days and weeks that followed their initial sexual encounter. Due to their positions in life, they each came up with different ways to rationalize their horrible actions of betrayal of a person each loved. Haley had less to lose from a social standing and nothing to lose from a financial standpoint in regards to her betrayal of her boyfriend. From a moral viewpoint, however, she clearly knew that what she was doing was wrong. She was betraying two people she greatly cared for and respected. Having an affair with a married man was wrong. Having an affair with the married father of her boyfriend was terrible. Having an affair with a close friend and mentor's husband, who also happens to be her boyfriend's father, was despicable. Haley grappled with the thoughts of her actions each day. But like Mitch, she was consumed with him almost as much as he was with her. Mitch represented everything that she had dreamed of as she was growing up in Bouvier.

Despite his previous bouts of infidelity, Mitch was not without personal shame when it came to this and his other affairs. All of his previous affairs had resulted in Mitch going into a period of depression. But not because because the affair had ended. The personal shame of his actions and his lack of self control had made him fearful of what he might potentially do later on in life. Each time he ended an affair, he swore to himself that this would not happen again. Deep down Mitch loved Clare. But his ego and his personal desire for instant gratification lead him down the same path again and again. If there were one shred of salvation for Mitch, it was that the time period between affairs continually increased as he got older. In fact, when he and Haley began their hot summer on the lake, it had been four years since his previous affair.

His last affair before Haley was such a disaster that Mitch swore to himself that if he could survive that dreadful situation he would never, ever stray again. He stayed true to his intent until the summer of Haley Fulz. The subject of his last affair was a long legged blond waitress named Misty Crews. Misty moved into town the summer before she met Mitch and immediately caused quite a stir in Bouvier. A single mother in her late twenties, Misty landed a job as a waitress at the Bouvier County Club. Her former husband had funded a very generous breast enhancement surgery for her shortly before their marriage was officially declared an irreparable disaster by a circuit judge in a neighboring county. Her natural looks, combined with her rather large breasts, which she displayed for all interested parties to see, made her an unbelievable attraction at the esteemed Bouvier Country Club. Within the first month of her taking the job, the club's lunch and dinner revenues began to soar as every guy in town wanted a peek at the new "hot chick." Additionally, every woman in town also wanted to see if this "hot chick" was really something that they should be worried about.

Upon first sight, every woman in town realized that Misty Crews was real trouble. They just didn't know exactly how much trouble she could actually be. This was something that Mitch McMasters unfortunately found out about in a very big way. Misty captured Mitch's attention from the first moment he witnessed her waiting on a neighboring table in the main dining room. Even though she was not supposed to be working his dinner table, Mitch informed the dining room manager that Misty would be his waitress that evening. One of the other waiters informed Misty that Mitch had money. She then proceeded to unbutton one more button on her already tight and very revealing sweater and made her way to meet Mitch McMasters for the first time.

Within two weeks of their first meeting, Mitch and Misty met at a secluded lake area resort, where they began their hot and contentious affair. Two weeks later, Mitch had to make his first loan of $1,000 to Misty to help her with some "unexpected emergency expenses." Three weeks later Misty needed another loan, only this time it was $5,000, which was soon followed by other loan requests of similar dollar figures. Little did Mitch know that Misty had two rather expensive problems. The first was a strong attraction to the local casinos in the state of Oklahoma, where Misty was a very bad blackjack player. The second problem was the cocaine and meth habit she had developed during her first marriage to a guitar player in an extremely loud and very bad rock band, named the Cockroaches. Both habits had caused her to rack up incredible debts to the type of people who didn't collect loans in the manner that your local bank would. The guys she was in debt to generally raped, broke bones, or took other more extreme measures in order to collect on their bad credit decisions. On top of her other problems, Misty also had several outstanding arrest warrants in the state of Oklahoma.

Because the sex between Mitch and Misty was so great and so frequent, Mitch continued to write the checks for the problem of the month until the price tab reached over $75,000. The final straw in their relationship was when Misty coaxed Mitch into making a trip across the state line to one of the numerous casinos that had popped up on the Oklahoma-Missouri border. The trip began well with some hot hotel sex in the casino hotel room and then some early luck at the black jack table. But soon after that things went down hill fast. Misty was spotted by some of the local muscle in the Miami, Oklahoma, area. Apparently, prior to her move to Bouvier she had stiffed some unforgiving Miami business people on an array of transactions which had included cocaine buys and prostitution proceeds, in which Misty had been performing sexual deeds for a variety of patrons in the Miami area. In fact, she was so good at her chosen trade that at one time Misty had been a virtual tourism industry for the Miami Greater Chamber of Commerce.

When Misty left the blackjack table to go to a restroom, little did Mitch know that his relationship was about to come to a hasty end. She was nabbed by some local goons who worked for some of the area loan sharks and pimps. While at the blackjack table, Mitch received an urgent phone call from a crying and weeping Misty. Between sobs she told Mitch that she owed some "bad guys" $25,000. And if she didn't pay it all tonight, they would kill her.

"What do you mean you owe some bad guys $25,000?" asked an incredulous Mitch.

"Mitch, I used to live here and I did some bad things. I owe these guys and they will kill me if I don't get them their money tonight. This is no joke, Mitch."

"What are you talking about, Misty?"

"Mitch, I used to have a gambling problem. I am in debt to some guys for my gambling." Misty conveniently left out the money she owed her pimp, a handsome sum for her impressive prostitution revenue. That would be have been a more difficult and challenging conversation that Misty didn't want to have to broach at this time in her life.

Misty explained that a large Hispanic man named Joaquin would be waiting for Mitch in the front lobby of the casino in fifty minutes. If Mitch gave Joaquin $25,000 in casino chips, she would be returned safe and sound. The next twelve hours resulted in Mitch being in debt to the casino for $25,000 only to leave town empty handed. A distraught Mitch discovered on the local news at seven o'clock the next morning that Misty had been arrested by the local authorities for a lengthy array of charges which included drug trafficking, bank fraud, armed robbery, and prostitution. Of all the charges, the prostitution charge was the one that hit Mitch's self esteem the hardest. Mitch McMasters had been messing around with a certified prostitute. He thought about how he could have sunk so low. Mitch also discovered from the news report that Misty Crews was one of several aliases she had been using.

Apparently after Misty, or whomever she actually was, had paid off her past sins, one of the goons, who happened to be an informant for the local cops, tipped off the cops to Misty's whereabouts. She was arrested at the bottom of a steep ravine on the edge of the Will Roger's Turnpike. Ironically, the discovery by the cops had been a blessing for Misty because she had been beaten and nearly left for dead.

Mitch McMasters left Miami a shocked and bewildered man, whose net worth was about $100,000 smaller as a result of his hot affair with Misty Crews. He secretly tracked Misty's legal troubles as they played out in the Oklahoma courts. The regulars at the Bouvier Country Club were curious about her whereabouts for a while, but as was the custom, they eventually moved on to other more pressing gossip. Misty was eventually sentenced to seven years in prison for her various crimes. The last news Mitch had seen about her was a news story which reported that Misty was scheduled to be out on parole in three months. Mitch hoped and prayed she didn't come back to the Bouvier area.

CHAPTER 4

THE memorial service for Haley Fulz would take place at the Bouvier Lutheran Church. Besides being the place that Haley had worshiped, it was also the only cathedral in town that was large enough for the expected crowd. The church was a beautiful southern styled building that was adorned with red brick and accented by large white columns. Not only was it the largest religious building in Bouvier, it was one of the largest in Southern Missouri. The long time pastor of the church was the Reverend Durwood Hardy. Hardy was a legendary religious figure in the Bouvier area. Over two decades he had built and maintained an impressive church following. Hardy was also renowned for surviving a scandal several years earlier. The scandal exposed an illegitimate daughter that Hardy fathered during an affair with one of his parishioners from a prior church over twenty years earlier. Hardy's wife at that time eventually died after being in a coma for several months. Her coma had resulted from a suicide attempt after Durwood's affair was exposed.

Several years after his wife's death, Hardy married the lady with whom he had the affair. He and his second wife, Veronica, built the church with their own donated funds as a testament to their commitment to the Bouvier community and Durwood's message that through God people could directly and indirectly impact people's lives by positive actions. Jackie Fulz knew that Reverend Hardy was the one person who could truly express the emotions being felt by Haley's family and friends through a message of hope, not hopelessness. Jackie had seen other community pastors in similar services before. Many times she had witnessed ill-equipped pastors leave mourners feeling more hopeless when they left the memorial service than they had felt when they arrived. She was confident that Durwood would strike the right note with those who loved Haley.

Surprisingly, Haley's father, Jake Fulz, had been very accommodative to Jackie since Haley's death. He even offered to pay for part of the funeral service; an offer that Jackie quickly and graciously accepted. Even though Jake had not set foot in a church in over twenty years, Reverend Hardy treated Jake with genuine kindness and grace.

After courageously beating leukemia, Durwood and Veronica Hardy's daughter, Mary, had joined Durwood in the ministry at the Bouvier Lutheran Church. Mary was diagnosed with leukemia at the age of twenty-one. After receiving a bone marrow transplant from her half sister, Caroline, and two years of various treatments, Mary was pronounced cancer free. She then decided to go into the ministry. Besides being naturally gifted, the cancer also gave Mary an unbelievable appreciation for life after being near death during her ordeal. She also provided comfort and strength to Jackie Fulz in a manner that only another female could. As good as Durwood was in his ministry, there were certain things that only a woman could truly communicate and convey to another woman in a time of great stress. Jackie felt blessed to have Mary Hardy by her side as she made decisions about the memorial service, decisions that she never envisioned ever having to make. After they had finalized the plans for the service, Jackie whispered to Mary that she would like to meet with Durwood and Mary without Jake.

Not long after Jake Fulz had left the church, Durwood and Mary welcomed Jackie Fulz into Durwood's church office. Durwood offered Jackie some fresh coffee. Jackie declined, but Durwood immediately filled himself a large cup of some new variety of Costa Rican coffee to which he had become addicted. Durwood had found that coffee, laden with lots of cream, and drinking bottled water were two excellent alternatives to stress eating. Stress eating had become all too common trait for Durwood. After maxing out at 235 pounds, he found the courage to start eating healthier. The coffee and water alternatives combined with daily walking had helped him shave thirty pounds off of his physique. Dressed in his customary blue blazer, Durwood Hardy and his full head of gray hair continued to be a striking figure, especially with the weight loss.

Jackie thanked Durwood and Mary for all that they had done for her and Jake. She sat in the office chair with her long blond hair pulled back in a manner that made her look younger and much more attractive than she normally did while working at the electronics factory. Even though the pressures of being a single mother and factory work had taken its toll on Jackie, her appearance today was evidence of her natural beauty. Jackie was wearing a nicely fitting pair of khaki slacks and a conservative white blouse. After an uncomfortable silence, Jackie said that she had something very painful and confidential to discuss with them. Jackie desperately needed someone to talk to at this painful time in her life.

"I received the results of the autopsy this morning. The doctor said that Haley died immediately at the moment of impact. If there is a bright spot in all of this, it is the knowledge that she didn't suffer. But the doctor told me something else, something that I could hardly believe. However, the doctor said that he is sure he is correct." Jackie began to cry and hesitated before completing her thoughts.

"Jackie, would you like to share with us what the doctor told you?" Durwood delicately inquired.

"Yes, but I ask that you not tell anyone. He said that Haley was six or seven weeks pregnant when she died. I just don't understand it. Chad has been gone all summer. If Haley was pregnant, then someone other than Chad was the father." Jackie sat there looking lost as she tried to retrace Haley's steps during the summer.

"Jackie, I know this is tough; but I think it may be important for you to try to talk to some of Haley's friends to see if they could offer some insight as to whom Haley was with this summer," Mary interjected in a manner that was both direct and kind.

"I know, I know. It's just tough talking to her friends. We all get so emotional when we get together."

"Jackie, I understand. But in the days ahead it will become easier to sit down with her friends. They loved her, and it will help them to be with you to talk about Haley. If you would like, I could set up a devotional and sharing get together in the next couple of weeks here at the church for you and some of Haley's friends." Mary's idea seemed to spark a rare glimpse of light in Jackie's eyes.

"Tomorrow, the sheriff and prosecutor want to meet with me and Jake to go over their accident report. Would either of you care to attend the meeting with me? It sure would help to have a helping hand there."

Before Jackie could complete her sentence, both Durwood and Mary eagerly agreed to go with Jackie to the meeting.

Durwood had developed a long friendship with Ernie Lambert, the prosecuting attorney for Barry County. With incredible assistance from Durwood, Lambert's career as a highly respected prosecutor was formed when he investigated the corrupt former Police Chief of Bouvier, the late Jack Buggle. Since that time Lambert and Hardy had become close friends, with each always looking for ways to help the other both personally and professionally. Having Durwood there would clearly provide a nice buffer for all parties for what would be a very emotional meeting.

Jackie went over a couple of more items for the service with Durwood and Mary before leaving the church. Despite the gravity of the situation, Jackie felt much better after spending time with the Hardys. Being able to have them with her at the meeting tomorrow with the sheriff and the prosecutor had calmed her nerves. Losing her daughter and finding out that she was pregnant when she died was almost more than Jackie thought she could handle. She knew that the Hardys would be there for her during the days ahead.

CHAPTER 5

AFTER examining the crash site for the third time, Sheriff Buford Blakeley had the feeling that he was missing something. There were too many pieces of evidence that didn't back up the initial theory that Haley had simply lost control of her car. Then upon further investigation of Haley's car, Blakeley found something that gave rise to his gut suspicions.

The back of Haley's car had the markings and a couple of dents that were not consistent with the other areas of the crashed vehicle. At this point Sheriff Blakeley decided to call on country prosecutor, Ernie Lambert, to pick his brain and to discuss his concerns and suspicions.

Ernie Lambert was in his eighth year as prosecuting attorney for Barry County. His career and his stature in the Bouvier community were transformed early in his tenure as prosecutor when he led a rape investigation of the then Bouvier Chief of Police, Jack Buggle. Until the time of the courageous investigation of Chief Buggle, Lambert had been seen by most Barry County patrons, and by Lambert himself, as an overweight, lazy, and underachieving attorney. The investigation of Buggle drastically changed the public's view of Lambert. Most importantly, it also transformed the underachieving Lambert into one of the most highly respected prosecutors in Southwest Missouri. For most of his professional life, Lambert had tipped the scales at more than 275 pounds on his five foot, five inch body frame. As his self esteem improved, so did his physique. Lambert lost over one hundred pounds and was clearly a different person, both from a physical and attitude standpoint.

As was their custom, Sheriff Blakeley and Lambert had to have a good lunch as a part of a serious discussion. Their favorite eating spot was Ruby's Pancakes and More. Ruby's was a legendary Bouvier café known as much for its great gossip as its food. It had always been a popular joint, but it had received a tremendous shot in the arm when it was purchased a couple of years earlier by a spunky former waitress and church secretary named Emerald Patrick. Patrick was another transformed soul who had been led to a better life by the influence of Reverend Durwood Hardy.

As Blakeley and Lambert made their way to a table in the back room of Ruby's, both could feel the energy in the room being focused on them. The Haley Fulz' car crash had dominated the café talk and town rumor mills. Now, the sight of Blakeley and Lambert together in the back room, of all places, would really send the Bouvier gossip tongues to wagging. But before they got to business, they had more pressing matters to tend to, specifically, which Ruby's entrée would they order today.

Since she was short a couple of waitresses, Emerald was busy waiting on her beloved café patrons today. The sight of the attractive and outgoing Emerald made both Lambert and Blakeley light up like a couple of love struck teenage boys. Emerald loved heaping attention on her customers and Lambert and Blakeley were clearly two of her favorites. In return they had been kind to some of her young and irresponsible waitresses when they had committed various minor offenses of the law. With a spunky smile that lit up the room Emerald approached the two mem.

"Well, I guess the owner of this joint serves any ole dog that walks in the door. What brings you two wayward souls to town? Wait, you must have heard about the incredible food of this joint, or did you just want to meet the owner? Do you boys want the special today?" Emerald stood before them, waiting for their smart ass replies.

"Emerald, I hope the foods gonna be good today because we sure as hell know the service won't be worth a crap," Buford siad with a little smirk awaiting Ernie to join in.

"Yea, why can't we get one of the cute young girls to wait on us, Emerald? The food always tastes better when that new one, what's her name, yea, it's Summer. When Summer, the brunette with the short skirt, serves the cornbread and the pork chops. It's almost like a religious experience." Ernie was quite satisfied with his reply.

"Well, boys I'm sorry I can't round up one of the cute ones for ya. If the local Sheriff would stop picking them up for every two bit offense in the world, I wouldn't be short handed. But I've got good news for you two today. If you are nice, unlike how you have been so far, I will see if the owner can fetch up some of today's special, barbecued brisket, corn on the cob, and cornbread that is fresh out of the oven. But you better hurry up with your orders and slow down with the offending words or the special will be sold out."

The mention of Emerald's barbecued brisket, corn on the cob, and hot, fresh cornbread make Ernie and Buford almost cry, especially the thought of possibly missing out on such a feast. They immediately shut up and ordered the specials.

Emerald smiled as they ordered. As she started to head to the kitchen, she stopped and asked, "Now, I better not see any peeks from you boys at my blouse or anything else since I apparently don't stack up to the young hot waitresses." She winked and gave them a wicked smile before heading away.

Ernie and Buford sat there and watched Emerald's adorable figure walk briskly to the esteemed kitchen of Ruby's Pancakes and More. For a few moments they remained silent as they soaked up the smell of Emerald's incredible perfume. They secretly wondered if the perfume was really that good or did Emerald's incredible aura make it seem that deliciously alluring.

Before they could devour their specials, Lambert and Blakeley discussed the grisly wreck. Blakeley reviewed his inspection of the wreck scene and the condition of Haley's car. He discussed the inconsistencies in the back section of the vehicle and the appearance of black paint on the rear bumper. Normally he would close the book on a wreck of this nature, but the dents and black paint were giving Blakeley pause before moving on to other matters in his department. After going over the various details, he asked Lambert his opinion. He valued Lambert's opinion more than any other in the county. The two had worked many cases over the past few years and had developed an important trust that was critical to the success of their respective law enforcement agencies.

"Buford, I can tell that you have a gut feeling about what you need to do. I've known you long enough that I can tell that there is something bugging about this wreck. And it's not just the age of the victim; it's something else. Am I correct in my assumption?"

"Ernie, initially it was a gut shot to see someone so young die in such a stunning way. These wrecks involving teenagers always hit me hard. But there is something else that doesn't make sense. Unless you think I'm just wandering around for no good reason, I'm gonna work this a little more. My gut feeling is that there is more to this than we know right now."

"I would check out some of the things that don't make sense yet. How about talking to her mom to see if she had been involved in any fender benders recently?"

"The car was virtually new. I am sure her mom would know if Haley had encountered any damage on her pretty new car."

"Buford, some of the girls in my office have been whispering around about how Haley came to own such a nice car. What's the scuttlebutt on the car?"

"Well, from what I have gathered, the car was a gift from the McMasters family for her graduation. She was going steady with Mitch's boy, Chad. And Haley was working for Clare at the paper. But I hear that the car did cause quite a bit of commotion at the high school and around town."

"Nice graduation present for a girlfriend. I hope my son's girlfriend isn't expecting a new car. Back in my day, a check for twenty five bucks or a travel alarm clock was the usual graduation gift, but a new car? It sounds like Mitch trying to show off, like usual."

Both shook their heads in disbelief. Their thoughts were immediately buoyed when they caught the sight of Emerald heading their way with two big brisket laden plates. Once again Emerald had given them the kind of hope that is normally the domain of talented evangelists or politicians. They dove in and for the next fifteen minutes forgot the troubles and pressures that filled their professional plates on a daily basis. Life was good when devouring Emerald's brisket, corn on the cob, and hot corn bread.

After they finished their incredible lunch, Ernie inquired about the autopsy.

"So Buford, I understand that Haley was pregnant when she died. I guess Mitch's boy was going to be the proud papa?"

"Ernie, I have not had a chance to talk to her mom about this yet. But from what I have picked up there might be a different turn on the proud papa question. So depending upon the age of the fetus, Chad McMasters may or may not be the dad. He has been over-seas doing the high brow studies this summer. Apparently, her red convertible was not the only thing she was riding this summer?"

Upon hearing that Ernie and Buford paused to let that thought sink in a little longer.

"Ernie, do the McMasters know about Haley's pregnancy?"

"Not to my knowledge. Haley's mom knows. But unless she has told anyone, she is the only person who knows besides us and the medical examiner."

Before they left the café, Lambert uttered the line that had been on both of their minds since they found out about Haley's death, "Buford, I know you are aware of this, but everyone is really upset about Haley's death. Because of everything involved with this situation, we have to get this right. A lot of people are watching. Give me a call anytime you want."

"I know, Ernie. I've told my guys that they better let me know anything they pickup on the street regarding Haley and what was going on in her life. I have a feeling that there is something lurking out there that is going to make us more than earn our pay from the fine citizens of Barry County."

CHAPTER 6

MITCH McMASTERS had tried to maintain as much normalcy in his life as he possibly could since the dreadful evening of Haley's death. For many reasons, he desperately tried to recollect what truly happened that night. Mitch had gone over the details of that fateful night with the same repetition that he had used many years earlier when cramming for college finals in courses that he had so arrogantly failed to attend. Now, Mitch keenly knew that this time a course grade wasn't on the line. No, this time his reputation, his family, and his future as a free, living person were all dependent upon his ability to collect his thoughts to the highest level of accuracy. One key question kept going through his mind. What did she leave behind that could bring me into this situation?

The day after the wreck he went over every inch of the lake house to make sure Haley had not left anything behind that would connect her with Mitch. Even though he felt as if he had done a thorough inventory of the cabin, he did find a little solace in the fact that if an article of Haley's were ever uncovered at the cabin, it could easily be passed off on her romance with Chad. Mitch knew that Haley had been to the cabin with Chad and their family numerous times before his perverted overtures entered Haley's life.

The thing that concerned Mitch McMasters the most was that the outcome of the fateful night with Haley was not planned. He had never laid out an elaborate plan to kill her.

To the contrary, he met her at the river cabin that evening in an effort to try to talk her through the news that she was pregnant and about her plans for the baby. More precisely, he wanted to talk Haley into aborting the pregnancy. Lord knows, Mitch had paid his way out of many problems in his life; and he had just chalked this up as one more of his examples of poor judgment and character that would come back to cost him dearly from a financial standpoint. After the episode years earlier with the call girl from Oklahoma, he had promised himself that he would never touch another woman other than Clare. But the positive dynamics of his relationship with Clare had diminished as his lack of attention and devotion to their marriage began to break down the valiant front that Clare had put up for years and years. The lack of consistent companionship with Clare combined with the fact that Chad was out of the country proved to be too much for Mitch when Haley came along with her gorgeous tanned long legs.

Leading up to the night of Haley's death, Mitch had received the dreaded call from Haley a couple of days earlier that she was, in fact, pregnant. After Haley had called him with the news, all he could think about were the words to the old Don Henley song, "I got the call today, I didn't want to hear, but, I knew it was gonna come." Deep down Mitch wasn't terribly surprised about Haley's pregnancy. Their affair had been so torrid that the thoughts of protection had rarely entered his mind except for after the deed had already been done.

Now that he was in a very real tight spot with regards to Haley's pregnancy, Mitch's plan was to sway Haley with promises of what he perceived as being genuine motivating interests for her. He was prepared to offer Haley the financial assistance to pay for all of her college education, monthly income while in college, and a new car when she became tired of the Honda Roadster convertible that he had purchased for her before they began their affair. But Haley was in no mood for his overtures that evening. She was beside herself over the pregnancy. The more Mitch tried to talk to Haley about what to do, the more agitated she became. Mitch mentioned that he would take care of her in any way she wanted or needed if she made their joint problem go away. This sent Haley over the top.

"So you are not going to be financially responsible if I choose to have the baby? Is that what you are saying?"

"Come on Haley, you know what I mean. You have so much going for yourself. I can help make so many things possible. How many girls your age have an opportunity to go to college without any concerns about how they are going to pay for it? If you want to study overseas during the summers, I can make that happen for you also. Look, just do what's right, and you can have so many doors open for you.

"I don't know what to do right now. I'm a high school senior, and I'm knocked up by my boyfriend's dad. I am so disgusted with myself I can't see straight. And to top it off you are now offering to put me up as if I'm some high priced call girl."

"Haley, you are taking this all wrong. I care for you and want to do this for you. If you want me out of your life, I will go. But I want to do this for you."

"What if I have the baby? Will you still put me through college?"

"Now, Haley, let's get your head turned around the right way. It's best if this problem goes away."

At this point Haley was crying uncontrollably. She didn't want to talk any longer with Mitch, but his arrogant manner was setting her on fire emotionally. She blurted out, "So what you are saying is that your generosity is available only if I have the abortion. From what I know from working the courthouse beat for your paper is that you have to support me if I have the baby."

"Haley let's not go there."

"Why not? I may want to have the baby. If I do, you have to provide support whether you like it or not. It's the law."

Since things were not going like he had planned and he was getting really ticked with Haley's lack of appreciation for his offer, Mitch turned beat red and yelled out the words he wished he could have immediately taken back, "Are you totally sure and totally confident that I'm the father? In other words, before you start making threats you better be sure you haven't been screwing anyone else this summer?"

When Haley heard those words she turned to Mitch with her teeth clenched and yelled, "I can't believe you. I can't believe you would think that I would do that to you. I'll see you in court, Mitch; you worthless bastard. Tell all your country club buddies that I am having your baby." Haley then ran out of the lake house, jumped into the Honda Roadster and sped off with gravel flying. A panicked Mitch McMasters didn't know what to do other than to go after her. He saw his life, his marriage, his relationship with his son, and the legendary standing of the McMasters family flashing before his eyes. Everything that he had deemed to be important in his life was now in the hands of an emotionally distraught, pregnant, eighteen year old girl who could easily wipe out his family's legendary standing in very short order.

The next few minutes seemed like a dreadful blur to Mitch. He remembered chasing Haley over the hills and curves of the road leading to the state park at speeds way too fast for two emotionally spent people. This was especially true for

Mitch, as he was trying to keep up with Haley while driving his black Jeep Grand Cherokee wagon, which did not handle curves well at high speeds. As Haley neared the state park, Mitch came over a hill at a speed of over one hundred miles per hour. Just as he crested the hill, Haley suddenly slowed down either out of fear for the rate that she was driving or to try to mess with Mitch. But it proved to be a fatal move for Haley because Mitch could not react fast enough to her sudden change in speed. His out of control vehicle bumped Haley's car just as it was at the peak of the road overlooking the state park. The bump apparently frightened Haley and she tried to overcompensate for the sudden movement to her car. She immediately jerked her steering wheel to the right and the next thing Mitch saw was Haley's car flying off the road. The drop from the road was so steep that he never saw the vehicle touch ground, but he could hear the horrific sound as it finally crashed violently into the hill over the park. Mitch felt unbelievably helpless, and he knew that she was dead instantly because of the horrific nature of the vehicle crash. He immediately pulled off the road and began to throw up. After regaining his composure, he drove into the park. There, Mitch found a pay phone, one of the few remaining in Barry County, and placed a call to the county's 911 center. He informed the dispatcher that he had seen a bad wreck on Roaring River hill. He tried to disguise his voice as best as possible. Mitch used a rag over the phone and used the best Yankee accent he could muster at the moment. He hoped and prayed that the 911 tape would never trip him up and never point to his traditional flat Barry County accent.

After placing the 911 call, Mitch headed back to spend the night at the cabin. He had done it so many times before during the fishing season that it would not send off any alarms with

Clare. She had resigned herself to his selfish and uncaring ways many years before Haley Fulz ever came along. But he was an emotional wreck and could not sleep. Finally, around 5:00 a.m., he dozed off only to be awakened by a phone call around fifty minutes later. At first he hoped that he had just encountered a horribly bad dream. But when he heard Clare's voice and the news that Haley was dead, Mitch knew that it was not a bad dream. His nightmare was very true and it would not be ending with his awakening from a very short night's sleep. Deep down, Mitch had a horrible, sick feeling. He knew that this nightmare was nowhere close to being over; in reality, it had just begun.

It was with mixed emotions that Mitch McMasters paced his river cabin. He was in mourning for someone he had loved dearly. Even though he tried not to admit it, Mitch had become as smitten with Haley as a seventeen year old becomes for his first love. Why else would he have risked everything to be with Haley? Now he was trying to come to terms with his need to cover up the death of someone whom he had craved so desperately. The first questions were the usual self criminations about why had he been so stupid to once again put himself in so much risk for public dishonor. To have an affair was dishonorable, but to have an affair with his son's girlfriend was a despicable act. An act that Mitch was now finally coming to grips with in the isolation of his river cabin.

There was no one whom he could talk to at this critical time of his life. Mitch had always been too self absorbed to have any close confidants, but he still had many people in town that he considered to be friends. However, he never really trusted anyone enough to be a true confident and the unseemly nature of this affair was definitely off limits to every one he knew. As he paced back and forth in the cabin, Mitch began to worry if the events would be too much for him to handle and remain a plausible figure to his family, associates, friends, and most importantly, to the police. He had seen the movies where a guy commits some horrible crime and then starts acting in various bizarre ways to those closest to him. The question that plagued him the most was would he really know and would he really be able to sense it if he was starting to act like a guilty party?

Finally, after what seemed to be an eternity of pacing, Mitch moved out of his temporary funk and started focusing on what he needed to do to cover his tracks effectively if the police decided to ask questions about Haley's death. But he was calmed somewhat by his belief that the Bouvier police would immediately wrap up Haley's death as an unfortunate auto accident and never pursue the matter any further. Mitch had never had much confidence in the Bouvier Police Department. Now he desperately hoped that his lack of confidence in their abilities would prove to be correct. Just as he began to calm down, Mitch was hit with the question that froze him in his tracks: had Haley told anyone else about the pregnancy? If she hadn't disclosed her condition, all he really had to contend with was the wreck report. However, he was fairly confident that the wreck would be classified as an accident. But if Haley had confided in anyone else, then he, Mitch McMasters, would be in for the challenge of his life.

CHAPTER 7

THE meeting with Jackie and Jake Fulz was something that Ernie Lambert did not look forward to, but it was necessary for the accident investigation. He wanted to be there to assist Sheriff Blakeley. The sheriff was as qualified as any Barry County Sheriff in recent memory, but Lambert sensed that his friend was a little intimidated by the fact that Haley Fulz was associated with the venerable McMasters family. Lambert did not share the same apprehension about Mitch McMasters. Through the years he had seen way too many examples of Mitch's blatant lack of character. He liked and respected Clare, but he thought that Mitch was a sorry son of a bitch who cared for no one but himself.

Ernie Lambert was dressed in his usual navy business suit, red and blue stripped tie, and white dress shirt. Since he had lost weight, Ernie tried to present himself in a more professional manner. His days as a fat slob are long gone, never to return as far as Ernie was concerned. He paced around his mahogany desk as he prepared himself for the meeting. The office was cluttered, but it was quite nice compared to most of his counterparts' offices. Behind his desk, sitting on the credenza were family photos, a photo of Lambert with the governor of Missouri, a funny photo taken of Lambert and Sheriff Blakeley in a dunking booth at a cancer society fundraiser, and a framed copy of a *Bouvier Gazette* front page article about Lambert bringing down a corrupt former police chief in Bouvier.

Anytime he was stressed about a delicate legal matter, which might involve an important citizen, Lambert would glance at the framed article. At the time of the famed investigation of the corrupt police chief, Lambert had virtually no confidence or experience in tackling a high profile case. Fortunately, with the encouragement of Reverend Durwood Hardy, he had found the guts to move forward. Since that time he had been very close to and felt very appreciative of Durwood Hardy for standing with him as he jumped head first into the famed inquiry. After the conclusion of the case, Lambert was seen by the citizens of Barry County in a totally different light. Years removed from the case, Lambert was one of the most respected leaders of the county. But he has never let the increased level of respect go to his head. As he became more confident and lost a bunch of weight, Ernie Lambert remained a good guy trying to do a good job for the citizens of Barry County.

As he glanced out the second floor office window, he could see the office building of the *Bouvier Gazzette* sitting regally on the town square. The sight of the red brick and white columned newspaper headquarters made Lambert wonder how Chad McMasters was holding up after the death of his girlfriend. Additionally, he knew that this had to be a terrible time for Clare as she had taken Haley under her wing at the paper. Lambert gave little thought to Mitch McMasters. Basically, he figured that since Mitch had little concern for anyone but himself, how could he be too preoccupied with the death of Haley Fulz. If Lambert only knew what was really going through the mind of Mitch McMasters at that time.

The meeting with the Fulz family concerned Ernie Lambert for many reasons. The first was that they had just lost their beloved teenage daughter and their grieving process has just begun. He knew that their emotions had to be all over the place in light of their situation. Secondly, they were going to have to discuss the horribly uncomfortable topic of Haley's pregnancy. Third, he could not give them an answer to the question regarding the wreck. Was it an accident, or did someone accidentally or deliberately run Haley off the road? He dreaded that part because it could take weeks or months to fully answer that question. And typically people want answers ASAP when it comes to the death of their loved ones, especially a teenager. Lambert had a sneaky suspicion that Jake Fulz could be a hot head. He hoped that suspicion was wrong even though his suspicions rarely were.

Jackie Fulz arrived first and she was immediately followed by Durwood and Mary Hardy. The sight of Durwood and Mary surprised Lambert, but he was instantly relieved to have them in attendance. If his suspicions about Jake Fulz were correct, having Durwood Hardy in the room could certainly not hurt matters. Typically, most people behave better than normal when they are in the presence of clergy. Lambert assumed that Jake Fulz would be no different.

Jackie Fulz was dressed in a summer weight floral dress that fit attractively to her small figure. It was evident that she had not slept much since the wreck as her face and eyes told the story of a very tired and emotionally drained person. She appeared to have aged ten years over the previous days. She sat down and politely declined an offer of a bottled water or soft drink. Durwood and Mary were casually dressed. Durwood was wearing his customary blue blazer along with his summer khakis and white short sleeved sport shirt. Mary looked amazing in her slacks, conservative pale blue top, with her pulled back hair. Ever though she was in her twenties, Mary Hardy had the elegance and grace of someone much older. Durwood accepted Lambert's offer of a Dr. Pepper. Durwood was nervous about the meeting, but you could never tell from his demeanor.

Jake Fulz arrived around five minutes after the others. He had just gotten off his shift with his employer and was wearing his work uniform. Jake looked old, tired, and in great need of a cold beer. Lambert could sense that Jake was uncomfortable being in a crowded room with his ex-wife combined with the circumstances of the meeting. But the tension subsided somewhat when Sheriff Blakeley walked in shortly after Jake Fulz arrived. The sheriff had been delayed by the usual assortment of matters under his direction: domestic disturbances, various fender benders, cows in the highway, and a meth surveillance operation that was getting interesting. After sitting down and receiving a cold bottle of Dr. Pepper, Sheriff Blakeley was ready to begin the meeting.

Lambert thanked everyone for coming to his office before turning the initial part of the setting over to Buford Blakeley. Buford stumbled around at the start of his presentation. The pregnancy topic and the sight of the Hardys were subconsciously intimidating Buford has he began to speak. He explained what they had found at the crash site, the approximate time of the wreck and the estimated speed that Haley was traveling when she left the road. The final item that he brought up was the sighting of black paint on the back bumper of Haley's car. With a band of sweat starting to build up on his rather large forehead, Buford reluctantly and hesitantly asked if Haley had been involved in any type of fender bender in the days leading up to the wreck. His question was met with blank stares and a muffled negative answer from Jake Fulz. As he asked the question, Jackie was thinking, "how in hell would Jake know anything about Haley's last days?" He had never been around or shown any interest in her or Haley for a long, long time. But she sat quietly and let Buford Blakeley continue with his clumsy presentation.

Burford cleared his throat, tugged at his shirt collar, turned red in the face and began to sweat even more profusely as he ventured into the territory he had been dreading all day long.

"I hate to bring this up. But since we are still investigating the wreck, I need to discuss one other item that came up in the autopsy. And folks I really hate to bring this up, but you never know if it has anything to do with the accident. Haley was pregnant at the time of the wreck."

Before he could go any further and sensing that he really needed some help, Ernie Lambert delicately stepped into the sheriff's initial question.

"Buford and I really struggled with this, but it could be relevant. The black paint on the back of Haley's car may or may not tie into the wreck, but it does get our attention. Do you know who was the father of Haley's child or what you know about the pregnancy?"

A red faced Jake Fulz looked around the room and with his eyes squinted, he began to speak. "So you're telling me that Haley was knocked up when she died. When did you find out about this?" Jake was simmering mad and was staring straight at Jackie when he let loose the first volley of what appeared to be the start of many more to come. However, before he could spew out anything else, Buford Blakeley showed the room what Ernie Lambert had known for a long time, his back bone.

"Jake let me just tell you something real quick like. If you talk to Miss Jackie or look at Miss Jackie in that manner again, I will toss your ass out of this meeting faster than you can bat an eye. She did a great job of raising Haley, so keep your damn mouth shut if you know what's good for ya." After he finished, Buford was afraid that he may have offended the Hardys; but when he glanced over at Durwood, he saw Durwood give a wink that tacitly said, "You did great, I totally agree!" Everyone held their breath, but they quickly realized that Jake Fulz had met his match. Jake hunkered down like a beat pup and wasn't heard from for the rest of the meeting.

Jackie Fulz delicately informed everyone that she did not know about Haley's pregnancy until the medical examiner informed her after the autopsy had been completed. Since she had found out, she had racked her brain trying to come up with who might be involved. To her knowledge, Haley had not dated anyone while Chad McMasters was away. She said that Haley's time was spent either practicing volleyball or working at the paper. Jackie added that Haley had put in a lot more hours at the paper during the summer, more than she had anticipated Haley would work on a summer job. As she made this comment, Lambert made a mental note to himself. He wondered if Jackie was just reciting the facts regarding Haley's employment or was there deeper meaning behind the statement.

Lambert asked Jackie for access to Haley's address books, cell phone, and other forms of communication that she might has used. He also asked for a listing of her closest friends. They would be delicately approached for Jackie to see if she could recall anything that might have been unusual in the days leading up to her wreck. Finally, Lambert inquired if anyone had made any threats against Haley or Jackie recently. Jackie sobbed as she shook her head.

At that moment Jackie appeared to be totally lost and confused with her circumstances. Just days earlier, her daughter was alive and had appeared to be the most wholesome and practically perfect child. Now, she was gone and Jackie was left with numerous unanswered questions and secrets about Haley's activities in the days and months leading up to her death. And possibly, her secrets may have brought about or caused her death. Jackie was in total disbelief about the turn of events in her life. She grabbed Mary Hardy's hand and held it tight as she sat quietly and sobbed for her daughter who would never come home again.

Even though it would take a considerable time for her to talk about it, Jackie was torn up about Haley not coming to her and talking to her about her pregnancy. The comment from the medical examiner, that she was about six or seven weeks pregnant when she died, was etched in her mind. Choosing to deal with it on her own was totally out of character for Haley. She and Haley had always been extremely close and had talked about things that most mothers and daughters didn't discuss. Jackie continued to think that if Haley wouldn't come to her about the pregnancy there had to be a deeper reason than the initial fright and shame that strikes a teenager when she gets the news that she is expecting. Deep in her soul, Jackie knew that the deep relationship she and Haley had was much too strong to let the news of a pregnancy stand in the way of their ability to lean on each other's shoulders. Because of this Jackie felt that it was terribly important for her to find out who was the father of Haley's child. If not for the purpose of the crash investigation, she needed to know for her peace of mind as a loving mom. With that on her mind Jackie, concluded the meeting by blurting out, "I believe as a mother that it will help answer a lot of questions if we can find out who the father is. Is there any way that could be determined?"

Lambert nodded and said that the medical examiner had preserved DNA samples of the fetus. If they found a credible lead on the father, testing could be done to identify him.

With that Jackie seemed the most relieved than she had since the news of Haley's accident. Lambert thanked everyone for coming. He and Sheriff Blakeley repeated promises to keep the family informed if they found out anything pertaining to the accident.

Just as Durwood Hardy was about to walk out of Lambert's office, Lambert whispered to Durwood that he wanted to talk to him briefly. Upon hearing this, Durwood turned around and Lambert quietly closed the door. In the presence of Sheriff Blakeley, Lambert stated that he had a feeling that Jackie Fulz' intuition was strong enough that she had a gut feeling or a solid idea about who the father might be, but she didn't want to say anything yet. Probably after she been allowed to properly mourn her daughter's death she would desire to open up and talk about what she knew or suspected was going on with Haley. Hardy agreed with Lambert's assessment. He stated that he and Mary would be in close contact with Jackie in the days ahead. Durwood felt that as Jackie moved through the grieving process, talking about her feelings would help her deal with her horrible loss.

As he was leaving Lambert's office, Durwood Hardy had a sick feeling that once the facts surrounding Haley's pregnancy became known, it was not going to be a pretty picture. He hoped he would be wrong, but he usually wasn't. Such was the life of a long-time, small town pastor.

CHAPTER 8

FRIDAY morning arrived, and it was the community's opportunity to say goodbye to Haley Fulz and to express their love for the girl who had excelled in all facets of her life. Normally a Friday morning in September was filled with talk about the Bouvier Cubs football game, to be played that evening, but today was different. The mood around town was somber.

It had turned into a beautiful September morning when the large crowd began to converge upon the Bouvier Lutheran Church. The sunlight reflected on the white columns of the church in a way that made it look like a scene from a movie. Inside the church, the cathedral was elegantly decorated for the service, with photos of Haley and her family, friends, and classmates. The Bouvier All Girls was placed in the choir loft while the church pianist played various overtures as the crowd filled the pews. Members of the Bouvier volleyball team were seated in the front row on the right side of the cathedral. Most of the volleyball team wore their letterman's jackets with the bold yellow BHS lettering on front of each jacket. The rest of the section filled quickly with classmates and friends. They all patiently sat in anticipation of the appearance of Haley's family and the McMasters family. At precisely 10:00 a.m., Durwood and Mary Hardy walked down the center isle of the church and gracefully asked for those in attendance to rise in honor of Haley's family.

Jackie Fulz took the first step of what seemed like a thousand mile walk as she began to make her way to the front of the church. She was attired in a black dress with a white scarf wrapped around her neck and shoulders. The color accented her natural beauty, which showed that day despite the strain and the tremendous grief. She was accompanied by her sister, a niece, and several cousins. Her parents had passed away several years earlier. Just five days earlier, she had sat in the same building with Haley by her side. At that time her daughter was excelling in virtually every aspect of her life and seemed to have her future planned for great success and happiness. Now, the past five days seemed like an eternity with all that had happened and what she had learned.

Jake Fulz sat at the opposite end of the front row than Jackie. Jake was accompanied by his brother Elvis and his sister Tiff. Tiff was appropriately dressed and appeared to have inherited nearly all of the family's limited stockpile of good looks and social graces. Elvis had made a mad dash into town, fresh off his coast to coast run for a regional trucking company. He forgot to get a pair of clean clothes and had to wear his trucking company blue work fatigues, which displayed more than a couple of grease spots on the shirt and pants and his name Elvis in bright blue letters. The grease on the clothes did match the grease in Elvis's long stringy hair. The attire and hair styling made Elvis look like he had just come off a casting call for an inmate for a prison movie. Apparently Elvis had inquired with Jake about getting a clean pair of khakis and a dress shirt for the occasion, but Jake didn't offer to help out with the purchase. Down to a few bucks in his wallet and a long trip back home, Elvis decided to dress as he was and bear the embarrassment and casting eye of attention of everyone in the cathedral. That was the case until the McMasters family began their walk down the church isle. Clare and Chad walked together holding hands. Both looked very distraught. Chad had the hollow look of someone who was in shock and didn't quite grasp their surroundings. He made his way to the church pew before he broke down in tears. The sight of her beloved son brought Clare to tears also. But Mitch McMasters looked the worst of anyone in the cathedral. The combination of no sleep, worry over his predicament, and genuine love for Haley had made Mitch look like a lost and bewildered soul. Most in the crowd were drawn to his features and his overall appearance. They had never seen the legendary Mitch McMasters look in such a way. It was noted by several in attendance that there was little, if any, type of contact between Mitch and Clare during or after the service.

After everyone was seated, Durwood Hardy rose to the church's glass podium, thanked everyone for coming to the service, and began to read Haley's obituary. He did so in a manner that added purpose and meaning to Haley's life. Durwood mixed in appropriate scriptures and showed how they applied to not only the occasion, but to Haley's life. In summary, he provided much needed comfort to Haley's family, friends, and loved ones. Durwood Hardy had summoned masterful performances in his career, but this was one of his finest.

The Bouvier All Girls Choir followed Durwood. They performed two numbers that they had perfected the prior school year. The final song was a beautiful and emotionally charged rendition of "Wind Beneath My Wings."

Mary Hardy gracefully came to the podium and began to talk about her experiences with Haley in the church's youth activities, which Haley had participated since she had been at least ten years old. She also shared the thoughts and memories of Haley that she had received from Haley's family and friends. The picture that was skillfully drawn by Mary's comments was that of a young girl who had achieved so much in her life, but the biggest achievement was her close relationship with her friends, family, and Christ. Then Mary, masterfully reminded everyone that no one, other than Christ, was perfect.

"Haley was amazing in so many ways. She was a great friend. And she was motivated to develop her God given talents each and every day. I loved to watch her tackle a project or pursue something that was important to her. She wanted to do her best and to make her mom, family, friends, and the Lord proud. Haley like all of us was a human being who could make mistakes. And fortunately, she had a wonderful way of learning from them, laughing at her failings, and using them to make herself better at what ever she was striving to achieve. But most importantly she loved the Lord, and she loved each and every one of you. And we are all better for having known Haley. When you were with her, she made you appreciate life because if anyone exemplified a full life it was Haley. And for Haley, a full life was seventeen wonderful years. Those seventeen years have been such a lasting gift from God. A gift that none of us will ever forget. We will all treasure this gift for the rest of our lives."

Mary added the line about mistakes at the last minute in hopes that it would ease the pain of those who might feel betrayed when they learned that Haley was pregnant when she died. She desperately hoped that Haley's legacy would not be tarnished by the events leading up to her death.

Once Mary concluded her remarks, the procession began for those in attendance to walk by Haley's open casket to see her for the final time. As it began, Jackie watched and marveled at the crowd that had gathered to pay their respects to her daughter. Seeing the pain on their faces and in their eyes became too much for her to bear and midway through the procession, Jackie gently placed her head down and stared at the floor for the remainder of the final good bye from Haley's friends and classmates.

Haley was laid to rest in a small country cemetery about three miles outside of Bouvier. She used to run on the road near the cemetery when she was in cross country. She had remark to her mom once about the beautiful setting for the cemetery. For this reason Jackie had chosen the Crestview Cemetery as her final resting stop. It was close enough to town that she could stop by Haley's grave anytime she desired.

As Jackie was leaving the cemetery the final person to hug her was Chad McMasters. Jackie could see the pain in his face. He promised to stay in touch. Jackie had always thought that Chad was a good kid and was thrilled when he and Haley started dating. She knew that some in town thought Chad was a spoiled brat, but to Jackie his words were sincere. Deep down she dreaded Chad having to find out that Haley had not been true to him in her final days. Jackie could sense that Chad had no idea of the secret that Haley carried with her to her grave. She too, wished she had never known. Her grandmother had once made the comment, "Sometimes it's best not to know everything about a person." Today Jackie knew exactly what her grandmother was talking about. Like Mary Hardy, she hoped that Haley's good works and her achievements would not be wiped out by a mistake of impulse or passion. But he also was keenly aware that in typical Bouvier fashion, Haley's achievements had created a large amount of jealousy, regardless how nice she had been to people. Because of this Jackie, sensed that in the final analysis, most people in town would focus solely on her indiscretion rather than her achievements and kind gestures. With that thought she stepped into the black funeral home limo and made the lonesome journey back to Bouvier, which would be the first of many without her beloved Haley.

The McMasters family rode together from the cemetery. After being able to compose himself, Chad sat next to his mom in the back seat of the family's black Lexus luxury sedan. The ride was quiet as no one really knew what to say at the moment or really wanted to talk after the agony of saying goodbye to Haley. Clare was trying to cope with the sadness and pain she could see in her beloved son. Plus, she had grown very close to Haley as she spent the summer working at the newspaper. The loss was especially painful as Haley had become the first person that Clare would talk to most mornings at the paper. Many mornings they would start things off with a walk to the donut shop on the Bouvier square for a fresh cup of coffee, hot Danish, and some of Bouvier's hottest gossip. Clare believed that Haley had the characteristics to be an excellent journalist.

In the mornings after the wreck Clare had caught herself a couple of times starting to walk over to Haley's work area, as had become her custom, for a quick chat to break up the work day. Clare knew that the tendency to look for Haley in the office would end, but at the moment is was another cruel reminder that her little friend wasn't coming back.

Mitch McMasters drove the Lexus back to town without speaking a word. Chad knew that his dad could have his "moments," as he used to call the time periods when his dad would be in a room purely from a physical sense, but his mind would be a million miles away. But he had never seen his father in as deep a trance as he was that day. Chad assumed that his dad was focusing on some business deal. Little did he know the true reason for Mitch's almost zombie like state that day.

Clare was also drawn to Mitch's off demeanor. Like Chad, she knew Mitch had his moody days; but this mood had been at this level for the past two or three days. She worried what he might be keeping from her. Was he in over his head financially on some land deal, was there another gambling debt, or had he snuck another bimbo into his life? Clare had vaguely known about two prior women. After some time of prayer and soul searching, she had forgiven Mitch after he confessed in a round about way. Clare was spared the gory details of the affairs, as she desired. She vividly remembered the time when a wayward husband confessed his extramarital sins to his Sunday school class in such excruciating detail that it made an already inappropriate Sunday school discussion go into the stratosphere for how not to handle a delicate matter. Despite his careful handling of the confession, Clare had told Mitch very clearly that she would not tolerate another affair.

Once they arrived home, Clare made a mental note to keep a closer eye on Mitch in the days ahead. Over the years he had developed a very loose routine, that had provided him with virtually no scrutiny over his daily activities and whereabouts. However, his demeanor and his total lack of regard for her and the family over the past few weeks made Clare either concerned or suspicious about Mitch and what he might be keeping from her. She thought to herself that maybe it was time to use some of her investigative journalistic skills on her own husband. But was she really prepared for what she might find out from her investigation? She thought of the Jack Nicholson movie line, "You want the truth? You can't handle the truth." Clare decided to forge ahead, regardless of whether she could handle it or not.

CHAPTER 9

IN the days that followed the memorial to Haley, Sheriff Blakeley took the crash investigation under his sole control. Though not uncommon in a small law enforcement department, Blakeley rarely handled an investigation that way. After conferring with Ernie Lambert, Blakeley decided that it would not be fair to Haley and her mom to have her name drug through the mud if the crash were the result of an innocent driving mistake by Haley. If it turned out to be something different, then Blakeley would have to go after all of the information at his disposal. After attending the moving service for Haley, Blakeley desperately hoped that he would learn that Haley simply made an error in her driving and that would be the only reason for her death.

One of Blakeley's first actions was to find out the information regarding Haley's pregnancy. This brought Blakeley to meet with Haley's doctor, Doc Josephson. Doc Josephson was a legendary character around Bouvier. He was a lovable scoundrel, who also happened to be a very fine doctor. Age had slowed down his tendency to chase women and drink too much bourbon, but he could still have his moments. Doc was lucky to still have his license to practice medicine after his second marriage ended in a divorce, but his ex-wife didn't use all she had in her arsenal. Getting caught giving a rather in depth and very personal vaginal exam of an attractive teenage patient was the final straw for his disastrous second attempt at marital bliss. The teenage girl wasn't smart enough to know that she could cash in on Doc Josephson's horrible lack of good judgment, but Doc's wife was. She was also smart enough not to go nuclear in the divorce, knowing full well that an unlicensed former doctor cannot pay much in the form of child support and maintenance.

Doc stated that when Haley found out that she was pregnant she was very despondent. She never offered up the name of the father. But she made it clear that the father would not be happy with the news.

"Buford, I've seen a lot of patients who had found out that they are pregnant. And I've seen almost every situation. You know, the young girl gets pregnant with her high school boyfriend, long-time relationship results in pregnancy, incest where the father has knocked up the daughter, and when a young girl is messing around with a married guy. Buford, if I were a betting man, I would bet that Haley was carrying the child of a married man."

"Now, Doc, what makes you think something like that? Have you heard something around town that I need to know?"

"Nope, I haven't heard a damn thing about this situation. But like I said, Buford, I can tell what's going on from my years of experience. This was an 'O Shit, I'm having a kid with a married, older guy' situation. When I confirmed the pregnancy, she said something like, 'This can't happen. It will ruin him.' But why are you nosing around talking to me. Didn't Haley die in a car accident? Are you suspecting foul play?"

With that question Buford Blakeley rubbed his chin, closed his eyes, and took a big breath that made his already rather large stomach protrude even further. "Doc, I don't know what the hell happened. Like you I have my hunches. And my hunch is that Haley didn't accidentally drive off the cliff over the park. Too many things don't add up."

"Did she commit suicide?"

"Doc, there isn't anything, other than it being a one car wreck, that leads us in that direction."

"She was pregnant and very, very down about her situation."

"I know, but the markings at the crash site appear more like an accident than an intentional drive off the cliff. When someone decides to intentionally drive off Roaring River hill, they don't hit the brakes. Haley hit the brakes and hit them hard before she went off the road. Plus, the back bumper of her car looks like it had been hit by a vehicle with black paint. According to her mom, Haley had never mentioned a having a fender bender. The line you mentioned, 'it will ruin him,' really bothers me. Shouldn't it, or am I reading too much into the comment?"

"I'm not a police guy, Buford. I think she was messing around with a married guy. But did that lead to her death? I don't know. That's why they pay you the big bucks." They both laughed. And then Doc Josephson's desire for gossip took over. "O.K., Buford, if she was messing around with a married guy, you have to have a few ideas about who might have been doing the dirty deed with that hot thing. Because Haley was certainly hot. And I know you well enough, you have to have some feelers out there that can lead you in the right direction."

"Doc, I don't know right now. I really don't. I hate to sully a young girl's reputation from the grave for no good reason if the pregnancy has nothing to do with her death."

"But Buford, you are too damn good at this not to have a hunch if you have a serious case involving the girl. Hell, you could have sent one of our flunkies out to talk to me. But you came out yourself. That tells me that you have a case, even if you can't officially classify it as a mysterious death. So who was she doing Buford?"

"Well, we can rule out the McMasters boy. He was in Europe or somewhere overseas when she got pregnant. Unless they've found a way to have actual sex over the internet, the kid is not the papa. So I've got to round up who she was doing during the summer. So she said, 'It will ruin him,' when she found out she was pregnant? That's pretty damn interesting."

"That's what I thought and that was before she died. Now that she's dead, I find it to be very interesting."

"She was working at the paper over the summer. I have considered going to Clare and ask her if she had seen anything. But I'm not so sure it would be a good idea yet."

Doc took a big draw off of his trademark cigar and let loose of a massive belly laugh that made his red complexion turn almost purple. "Buford, are you kidding? You are going to march in and tell Clare McMasters that Haley was not only stepping out on her son while he was in Malaysia, or wherever the hell it was, but she also got pregnant in the process. Now, that is going to go over really well, especially when she tells that arrogant husband of hers. If they think you are going to tarnish their polished reputation and make their family look bad with this investigation, Mitch will find an opponent to run against you in the next election. And he will write lots of sweet editorials about your opponent. Buford, I have seen their pride in action, and it ain't pretty. Hell, they gave the girl a shinny red sports car and then she starts screwing someone else as soon as Chad hits the airport to fly to wherever the hell he went last summer. Trust me, they will do anything to keep their precious little Chad from being disgraced by a wayward girl friend, especially a dead one. Until you can tidy up your loose ends, I would avoid the McMasters as much as possible."

"Thanks a lot, Doc. The thought of having to campaign again for this damn office is a real charming notion, especially after two straight elections without an opponent. You are probably right. But if things turn out like I suspect, the day will come where I have to sit down with Clare and Mitch. Man, that will be a real treat. You want to say anything else to brighten my day before I head out of your God forsaken office?"

Buford and Doc shared a good laugh before Buford headed out the door. Buford felt a little better after talking to Doc. Doc Josephson was one of the few people in Bouvier that Buford Blakeley could talk to confidentially and not have the conversation spread all over town within fifteen minutes. Plus, Buford considered Doc to be one of the wisest guys he had ever met, except for his penchant to chase women. But those days had waned greatly with age. He was also one of those guys who would tell you the truth even if it was something you really didn't want to hear.

Each Wednesday evening, Mary Hardy led an enormously popular bible study for students in Bouvier at the Bouvier Lutheran Church. Most of the students in the setting were of the ages fourteen to eighteen years old and most were female. As Mary learned a long time ago, if you had pretty girls attend a bible study, it was amazing how many young boys started getting interested in the bible. The fact that Mary was a stunning young lady certainly helped attendance by the young boys as well. The Wednesday following Haley's memorial service, Mary Hardy could feel the tension in the youth meeting room. Adorned with bright colors, motivational quotes, and attractive photos of various members of the group scattered along the walls, the youth room had a warm and inviting presence. Two leather sofas and several padded chairs gave those attending a comfortable seating arrangement. Mary had designed the room so that it would be less intimidating than the traditional church meeting room and provide a warm atmosphere for the youth involved in the church programs.

Haley had been a long-time and very active member of their class. Her absence was definitely felt by everyone in the room. Her ability to discuss the bible and how it applied to the life of an average teenager would be missed. Second, the knowledge that she was never coming back permeated throughout the room. It wasn't like she was gone for just this week. Haley was dead, and her death had had a profound impact on everyone in the room. Sensing this, Mary announced in the Bible study that evening that if anyone needed to discuss what they were going through after Haley's death, she would be available to talk to them anytime they desired. After making the statement, she could see that it had made its mark as several of the girls looked down and then their eyes filled with tears.

Once the evening's class drew to a close, three girls around Haley's age caught Mary in the hallway and asked if they could talk to her in the privacy of her office. Mary led them to her office where she closed the door and offered them soft drinks. All three declined Mary's offer. Mary knew that all three of the girls had been close to Haley through their interactions in the church youth activities.

The first girl to speak up was Lizzie Nicholas. Lizzie had been Haley's best friend for many years. They had been virtually inseparable as they spent most of their free time in volleyball or choir practice. Lizzie was seventeen, tall for her age, and very attractive with flowing naturally blonde hair. Even though she wasn't as pretty as Haley, Lizzie never had trouble getting a date, when she wanted one. But she prided herself on her grades and her achievements in volleyball and choir, so boys typically took a backseat to her ambitions.

Lizzie considered herself to be poised; but as she began to talk about Haley her composure began to wilt and tears welled in her eyes. She paused long enough to regain her voice, and then she began to explain what she had witnessed in Haley's last days.

"Something happened to Haley shortly before she died. During the later part of the summer, she would go days without contacting us, which was totally out of character for Haley. We used to talk three, four, or five times a day. But then once school started up she was distant and withdrawn. Then the day before she died, she came to me and said she needed to talk. She said that it was something that was very, very personal; and I had to promise to never tell a soul what she was going to tell me. I was stunned when she began to tell me her story. And I feel horrible repeating it now because I promised Haley. I have kept my promise until now." At this point Lizzie's flowing blond hair was as much a wreck as her once prized composure. She was conflicted over her pledge to her dead friend and her desire to provide information that might lead to closure for Haley's family.

Sensing that Lizzie needed a break, Mary walked over to her chair, placed her arm around Lizzie's shoulder and let her cry, knowing that she was there for her. Lizzie's two friends tried to help console her and encourage her that she was doing the right thing to discuss what was going on in Haley's life at the time of her death.

Mary then began to softly speak to Lizzie. "Lizzie, I know you loved Haley. All of you did. Haley loved you guys more than you will ever know. Sometimes we don't know what to do to help someone. Sometimes we get overwhelmed and don't know what to do to help ourselves. It sounds like Haley may have been in that position when she came to you. She trusted you, and she needed help. Talking about our problems is the first step to getting help and solving our personal dilemmas. Haley is gone. But we can still be there for her. We can still help her family. And the way we can help is by talking about our love and our memories of Haley. The other way is to talk about things that we know that might help the sheriff determine what happened the night Haley died, because they don't know for sure what happened. And I know that for Haley's mom to have closure knowing what happened is the key for her to be able to move forward. To be blunt, she desperately needs to know whether Haley's death was an accident or did it happen on purpose."

Mary's talk helped Lizzie's composure. "You are right. Telling what she told me might actually help. I guess that is for the Sheriff to decide, not me. O.K., Haley said that not long after Chad left for Europe, she began to see a man that she had been infatuated with for some time. She said that he was successful, handsome, charming, and had all of the things or possessions that would catch a girl's eye."

"What type of things or possessions was Haley talking about?"

"She said that he had numerous cars, one was a sports car. He aslo had a couple of boats, a lake house, and a very successful business. But he also had a wife and about twenty five or thirty more years of age than Haley. She said she felt horrible about falling for someone who was married and for all the wrong reasons. What she meant was she was drawn to his rich lifestyle. And that had not been the way Haley had normally approached life, except for her attraction to Chad. We never understood the Chad thing, other than he possessed all the things the married guy also had. Chad was pretty good to Haley, but he could also be a condescending jerk at times. I know he joked around to some guys before he left for Italy that he couldn't wait to lay some hot Italian chicks this summer. I'm pretty sure Haley heard about the comment after Chad left town."

Mary gently began to ask Lizzie some more detailed questions about her last conversation with Haley. "Lizzie, how would you describe Haley's demeanor when the two of you last spoke?"

"She was very down. After telling me why she was attracted to this married guy, she began to cry uncontrollably. Before she pulled herself together, I was getting afraid that she was having a nervous breakdown. She was in a really bad state of mind. She kept saying over and over, 'This can't be happening; this can't be happening. I can't believe I'm in this position. I feel so guilty for what I've done.' I said that she should just stop the affair now and hope no one ever finds out. Then she dropped the bombshell on me. She said that stopping the affair wasn't as easy as it sounds because she was pregnant with the married guy's kid."

Mary sat there trying not to act like she already knew what she had been told; but at the same time, she didn't want to be a phony and act totally surprised either. As usual, Mary handled the situation perfectly. She quietly said, "I see," and nodded her head in a manner that gave Lizzie the sense that she understood the enormity of the situation. "Lizzie, did Haley ever tell you who she was having the affair with or the name of the father of her child?"

"She wouldn't tell me right then. But she said that she would when the time was right. She first needed to talk some things over with him before she wanted to say any more. She begged me not to tell anyone, especially her mom. I don't think she had known about the pregnancy very long."

"Did she discuss her plans for the baby?"

"You mean, was she going to keep it? Yes, she intended to have the baby. Anymore, lots of girls get in this position are able to make a life for themselves."

"Lizzie, did she tell you whether the father felt the same way as she did about having the baby?"

"No, no, no; she had not had that discussion with him. Haley said that she was dreading telling him of her decision to keep the baby, because with him being married and all that, she knew that he would not be happy."

"When was she going to tell the guy about her decision?"

When Mary asked the question, Lizzie broke down again. Between sobs she was able to softly speak, "She was going to tell him the night she died." As she spoke those words, Mary's stomach developed a sharp knot. Even though she was not surprised by the answer, hearing it confirmed her worst suspicions, that Haley either intentionally drove her car off the mountain, or she was forced off the road and crashed. What she had just heard was confidential information that could not be shared unless Lizzie authorized its release. But Mary instantly knew that the Sheriff and the Prosecutor needed to know about Lizzie's story. Reluctantly, Mary asked Lizzie some additional questions.

"Lizzie, what you have told me I know had to be terribly painful to discuss. I know you loved Haley and she loved you. Even though the last couple of months were not the same as they had been in the past, it still doesn't take away the bond you and Haley had. The fact that she trusted you enough to share her secret with you clearly demonstrates that bond. You know I said earlier that we can still help Haley even though she is gone. Well, Haley needs our help. She needs the truth to come out about what happened to her on the mountain. I get the feeling that her wreck wasn't an accident. I am not privy to any wreck site information. My feeling is the sense a person gets when they work with people each and every day and hear their stories. You can sense if something isn't right. And I have to be painfully honest with you; I get the sense that we must find out exactly what happened with Haley the night she died. We all loved Haley. If someone did harm her, then that must be investigated. And to properly investigate, the Sheriff must know all of the information regarding that night."

"Mary, do you think I need to tell the Sheriff what I know?"

"Yes, he really needs to know what you told me."

"O.K., but would you care to go with me? I've never talked to a detective before, and it really freaks me out, especially considering it's about Haley."

"You bet I will be there with you. And if you need to talk about anything else, just call me anytime."

Mary breathed a big sigh of relief knowing that Lizzie would agree to talk to Sheriff Buford. She then turned to the other two girls in the room, Morgan Langley and Kate Johnston. Like Lizzie, Morgan and Kate had been long time friends with Haley. Morgan was very quiet. She was a very attractive girl, with long black hair, a figure that would give someone the impression that she was much older than seventeen, and piercing blue eyes. She sat in her chair with her legs crossed in a manner that gave the impression that she was not as comfortable being in the room as the other two. Kate was a very energetic blue eyed blond, who gave the impression of being a party girl. This was partly because she dressed the most provocative of the three and also due to her past as a happy girl looking for the next party to crash. Her parents owned a resort on the lake near Castle Rock, so there was always a social outing of some type taking place on the lake during the summer. Before Haley, Kate had dated Chad McMasters until Clare deemed Kate to be less than acceptable for the McMasters' style. However, after starting to attend the youth sessions at the church with Mary Hardy, Kate had made great strides in slowing down her temptations to party hardy.

Kate seemed ready to talk after Lizzie had cleared the air. "Haley was really different the last part of the summer. It was totally unlike her to blow us off when we were planning to go to the movies or boating or things like that. But wham, around the middle of the summer, she kind of shut us out. First, I got the impression she had gotten the big head because of the car, but we all started thinking that there was something else going on. So I have to admit, I started snooping around. You know Bouvier; it's really tough to keep a secret in this gossipy town. I started asking some questions. You know, if anyone had seen Haley, stuff like that. You ask the question enough, it's amazing where it will lead you. Morgan and I started getting suspicious. We left Lizzie out of it because she was too busy with her volleyball stuff. And she was too close to Haley. We didn't know she was going through the same stuff with Haley that we had. We followed Haley a couple of times when she left the newspaper. Where she was going is not good. Not good at all, especially with what Lizzie has just told us. We followed her, and we also took my parent's boat and drove it by the place she was staying most evenings. One night, we caught a glimpse of her on the deck of the lake house with the mystery guy. After seeing what we saw and hearing Lizzie's news, ladies we are playing with fire. I know Lizzie is willing to talk to Buford. But until my parents say its O.K., I'm not going near this. With what I know and Lizzie knows, this could be the biggest scandal to hit Bouvier since, uh well, in a long, long time."

Mary took Kate's near faux pas in stride. She knew Kate was referring to the scandal several years earlier involving her mom and dad, when the news hit that the Reverend Hardy had fathered a child out of wedlock. Mary felt that supporting Kate was the best route to take.

"Kate, I know what you are thinking. And it is perfectly normal to fear bringing something out in the open, especially if it is something very sensitive. I think that it would be wise to talk to your parents about this and get their feedback. If it might impact them, you want them to know. They can give you guidance for how to deal with something that is sensitive and potentially fearful. What do you think you parents will say when you talk to them about this?"

"I don't think it will go well. The guy involved knows my dad well. They are not close friends, but they play golf and socialize together. My dad's social circle is very important to him and his image. He said it helps our resort business. If I were to come forward with my information, it would really mess up his standing in his little social clique, if you know what I mean. I love my dad, but he associates with a lot of shallow, self important jerks, to be brutally honest. And the guy with Haley is the king of the gang. So I think you get the drift about how big this could be if it got out about Haley's affair with this guy."

"Kate, you are exactly right to be concerned about your dad's reaction. How will your mom feel about this?"

"Funny you asked, because mom is friends with the wife. Yes, the wife of the guy who was messing around with Haley. Mom's social clique is almost as important to her as dad's is to him. I can guarantee you that mom will tell me to keep my mouth shut. I mean, this couple that is tied to Haley's affair is very influential in this town. They are the last people you want on your bad side."

As Kate finished, Mary could sense the tension in the room. She could tell that Kate was conflicted about what to do, but she feared the wrath of her social butterfly, materialistic parents. Mary didn't know Kate's parents; but from Kate's description, she had the distinct idea that she would find them to be very dislikable. She had seen the type before. They sounded like the prototypical type who place their social standing, their little clique, and their social calendar ahead of everything, especially the interests and desires of their kids.

Biting back her distain for the description of Kate's parents, Mary stated, "Kate, what I would recommend is that you pray about this situation and ask the Lord for direction. You are very thoughtful of your parent's needs. But I ask you to also consider, what do you think is the right or just thing to do. Sometimes the right thing to do is also the toughest thing you will ever have to do in life. I have seen many people who have said that doing the tough things made them better because they could go on with their life with a peace of mind knowing they did what was best. Even if it wasn't pleasant at the time, they went through with the decision. Does that sound fair enough, Kate? And remember, you can talk to me anytime you desire."

Kate nodded to Mary, but all present could tell that Mary's mild rebuke had not hit the right cord with her. Kate folded her arms and waited for Morgan to speak. In a matter of minutes, the happy, energetic party girl persona had disappeared and had been replaced by a young girl who was conflicted and sulking because of her situation.

It was now Morgan Langley's turn. But grasping the tension in the room, especially Kate's angst, she declined to elaborate beyond what Kate had already said. Kate had implicated her in her knowledge of Haley's romantic partner, and she did not deny anything Kate had said. Mary got the impression that Morgan's parents probably had ties to the person involved with Haley. Morgan's dad was an executive with a large transportation company, and her mom was a school teacher at Bouvier High. But Mary also got the impression that Morgan's parents were not tied to the same social clique as Kate's parents and that their social standing held less importance. Morgan seemed to be more genuine and down to earth. In fact, she gave the impression of being quite shy.

Sensing that all involved were tired and talked out, Mary closed their session with a short prayer. As they left, each one of the girls hugged Mary and thanked her for listening to them. Kate whispered to Mary that she was sorry for not being able to talk to the sheriff yet. Mary gently whispered back that she understood and that everything would be fine.

After the girls left, a drained Mary called her dad and informed him that she sensed that a real mess was going to be uncovered when the Sheriff looks deeper into Haley's death. Mary said she was heading home, but asked her dad to meet her for breakfast. She was having a strong desire for a strong coffee and some biscuits and gravy to start the next day. Durwood was more than happy to comply with his beloved daughter's request. His mind raced for over an hour about what Mary had found out about Haley. But he knew that he would definitely have no trouble rising the next morning.

CHAPTER 10

YOU COULD smell the bacon frying a mile away and the aroma of the fresh hot coffee was just as inviting for the patrons of Ruby's Pancakes and More on a crisp Thursday morning in September. As Durwood and Mary made their way to a booth in the back section, they passed by the legendary long dining table, also known as the board of directors table, where the farmers, ranchers, law enforcement officers, and regular good ole boys gathered for their morning breakfast, and just as important, hot Bouvier gossip. Polite acknowledgements were made by most parties as Durwood and Mary passed by the board table. Most at the board table didn't care for Durwood, as they found him to be too slick and perfect for their liking. Durwood had long become accustomed to their perceived stereotype of him and no longer cared if they liked him or not. Deep down he realized most of their dislike came from jealousy of his accomplishments in the community. Mary always caught their eye. Her beautiful figure combined with her vibrant personality always caught everyone's attention. The regulars at the table really liked Mary. She was always polite and kind to the group. But she was keenly aware of their feelings for her father, which did not sit well with her at all.

Durwood was delighted to see Mary. They were seated in a booth that afforded them some greatly needed privacy. Or, as much privacy as they could expect at Ruby's. Once they were seated, Emerald Patrick, the owner of Ruby's, rushed over to see her favorite customers. Emerald readily credited Durwood for saving her from a self destructive life and was always delighted to see the Hardys in her establishment. She gave Mary a hug and then gave Durwood a peck on his cheek.

Emerald livened things up by reciting from memory their usual breakfast routine. "Now, Mary, I know your fired up for some biscuits and gravy served with some fresh hot Costa Rican coffee with a touch of cream." Mary nodded in approval of not only Emerald's correct assessment of her breakfast desires, but also in amazement of Emerald's infectious personality. Emerald then turned to Durwood. "O.K., this will be a little harder, since he always tries to trip me up. Rev, I'm betting today that you are hungry for the pecan pancakes, maple syrup, a side of hash browns, and some Costa Rican coffee with lots and I mean lots of creamer."

Durwood sat there for a moment with a smirky smile as he tried to decide between the biscuits and gravy or the pecan pancakes. He knew that he couldn't go wrong with either selection. After a couple of moments of hesitation, Durwood chose the pecan pancakes. "You know Emerald, you are amazing. I came in dead set on getting the biscuits and gravy, but the thought of the pecan pancakes was just too much to pass up. Hey, did you say anything about lots of cream in my coffee?"

Emerald playfully slapped Durwood in the head with the menus as she said, "No, I didn't realize you like lots of cream in your coffee. We will make a note of that in the kitchen. In fact, we have hired Harley Jones to bring in one of his dairy cows to hang around for the days you drop by for coffee."

Everyone in the café heard that line and enjoyed it at Durwood's expense. Durwood loved it also. He especially loved the sight of Emerald doing what she loved and making a positive life for herself. He marveled at what she had accomplished in a few short years removed from her destructive past. The fact that the café was smoke-free and still packed said more about Emerald and her ability to connect with people than anything else. When she purchased Ruby's, the first thing she did was make it smoke-free. All of the regulars threatened to walk out and never come back. But Emerald's personality, looks, and the great food enticed all of the regulars to come back and to stay.

Durwood looked at Mary and said, "I can tell you didn't sleep well last night. I can tell by your eyes."

"You are right. I'm glad you were free this morning. I really needed to talk to you, and a Ruby's breakfast sounded really good. Is Mom going to make it for breakfast?"

"She was sleeping in, but said she would try to get around to join us in a little bit. Now be honest, the thought of a Ruby's breakfast was probably more inviting than getting to see me."

They both chuckled, and Mary simply said, "Dad, you are mess."

After getting their much desired Costa Rican coffees, Durwood was ready to hear about the bible study from the night before. "Ok, tell what happened last night. Your phone call definitely got my curiosity stirred up."

"Well, Dad, do you know any of the girls that hung out with Haley?"

"The girls that I am familiar with are the three that attend your bible study. First, there is Lizzie Nicholas; then Morgan Langley; and the party girl Kate Johnston. Lizzie's mom, Natalie, attends the late service on Sundays. I believe her dad lives in Wichita at this time. Her parents haven't divorced, but it doesn't look good for them at this point. Morgan's parents, Chase and Olivia, attend the second Sunday service off and on. And Kate is Pate and Madison Johnston's daughter. I don't think I have ever seen Pate and Madison in the church. From what I hear, Pate is usually patching up his hangover around the time church service would be starting."

"Dad, let's be nice; you know what the bible says about gossip."

Durwood chuckled, shook his head, and continued, "I know, I know; it's my one vice: gossip. To be honest I have been around Pate Johnston on a couple of social occasions around town. He is a long day. You know the type, a major blow hard, very obnoxious, every conversation centers around him, his resort, or his golf game. To give you a better example, he is just like his running buddy, Mitch McMasters." As soon as he said Mitch McMasters, Durwood knew that he had hit a nerve with Mary. The look on her face was a kind of sick look of dread. Durwood glanced at his beautiful daughter and said, "O.K., I can tell that I just said something that didn't sit well with you. I assume it has to do with you learned last night."

Mary paused, ran her hands through her hair, and then casually looked around their seating area to see if anyone was within earshot. Seeing that she was free to talk without being overhead, she began to explain the summary of her talk with the three girls the previous night. The more she talked, the more Durwood came to realize why Mary felt the way she did. He knew Mary's instincts were right on when she made the comment, "I think a real mess is going to be uncovered when the Sheriff looks deeper into Haley's death."

Like Mary, Durwood had taken the knowledge from Lizzie about Haley being pregnant with a married guy who was successful, handsome, and had all of the things or possessions that would catch a girl's eye, including a lake house, and a very successful business. Plus, the information from Kate about seeing Haley at a lake house of someone who ran in her father's same social clique, combined with the remark.

"She said that he had numerous cars, including a sports car. And he had a couple of boats, a lake house, and a very successful business. Plus, she made the comment that Haley's lover was the king of the clique and to poke around the affair would be like playing with fire. Durwood certainly knew who the king of Pate Johnston's clique was, and it was none other than Mitch McMasters. After hearing all of this, he was confident that he and Mary hadn't taken two plus two and had come up with sixty-four. No, he was confident that they were exactly right in their gut feeling regarding the father of Haley's baby. However, the hard part would be how they handled what they knew. Specifically, how would they get the information to the sheriff and the prosecutor without violating pastoral privilege and without incurring the vengeful wrath of Mitch McMasters and his support cast?

"Mary, we have to be very careful and walk the line of helping Lizzie step forward with what she knew and not cross over the line and violate the pastoral privilege of confidentiality. From what you said, Kate Johnston is not going to come forward. But the information will come out sooner or later. In Bouvier it always does leaks out. We have to be precise in our communications with Buford and Ernie and keep a log of our conversations, because Pate Johnston is the type who will sue you if he thinks he can make a buck."

"Ok, ok, so I take it that you will not be inviting Pate Johnston on the church's men's canoe float trip next summer. I will keep a log of any conversation I have with the girls and with Buford and Ernie. How should we proceed from here?"

"I will call Ernie Lambert and I will let him know that Lizzie wants to talk, but I won't give him any details. It will be best if she talks just to Ernie and Buford. I think Buford has some moles in his department, some guys who are more than willing to sell important information, if they have the chance. And I suspect Mitch McMasters would be more than willing to pay a fair price for any information being possessed by the Sheriff's department. You know he has to be sweating some bullets right now. Even if Haley's death is a pure accident on her part, the thought of the news getting out that she was having an affair with Mitch McMasters just makes your head spin. With all the wrongs, it has the potential to be the biggest scandal in Bouvier's storied history. It would certainly knock me off the charts. And I'm not comparing sins at all. I'm talking strictly from a standpoint of the McMasters being Bouvier's most famous family. That combined with a father having an affair with his son's girlfriend makes it a combustible bomb ready to detonate. And we haven't even thrown in the mysterious death of the pregnant girlfriend. The real question will be whether Clare and Chad turn on Mitch. You were right, Mary, this is going to get ugly. So let's be careful."

"What about mom? She and Clare McMasters are pretty close."

"I won't go into everything, because your mom doesn't like to be privy to confidential matters. But I will give her a heads up that Haley's death will more than likely open up some things that we couldn't imagine, and the McMasters are deeply involved. She will understand the situation and will never say a word to anyone."

"Thanks, because I didn't want mom to be blown out of the water by the allegations and be caught in an uncomfortable situation with the McMasters."

"Exactly, I appreciate your concern. Speaking of your mom, here comes the gorgeous Veronica Hardy herself."

All heads in Ruby's turned as Veronica Hardy made her way to Durwood and Mary's table. She had always been a controversial figure in Bouvier for several reasons. The first had been way in which she became known to citizens of Bouvier. The affair between Veronica and the Reverend Durwood Hardy produced an out of wedlock baby, Mary. The existence of the affair was kept secret for over twenty-one years, until Mary was diagnosed with leukemia. Durwood's wife, at the time, ultimately died from a suicide attempt when she was told of the old affair and the daughter that had resulted from the affair. Needless to say, Veronica Hardy had many hurdles to overcome when she and Durwood married and she moved to Bouvier to become a pastor's wife.

Veronica however, was no ordinary small town pastor's wife. Prior to marrying Durwood, she had made millions in various business ventures in Branson, Missouri. Her most famous and lucrative venture was her ownership of a music theatre on the strip in Branson At that time her show was Branson's most popular and successful country music venue, which featured a fabulously talented singer/comedian who specialized in a Frank Sinatra parody under the stage name of "Frank Bransonatra." After marrying Durwood, she divested herself of all of her outside financial holdings and focused solely on Durwood and their ministry. The Bouvier Lutheran Church cathedral was funded in a very large part by a very generous donation from Durwood and Veronica. Additionally, having been an unwed mother and having dealt with the challenges of raising Mary on her own, each year Veronica funded scholarships to several Bouvier High School graduates who have become single mothers prior to their graduation. The recipients must maintain a high grade point average, stay off drugs and alcohol, and agree to attend a college in the state of Missouri. The scholarships fund not only the student's tuition, housing, books, and daycare; but they also provide a part-time job at the Bouvier Lutheran Church. Although controversial at the time of its inception, the scholarship program has been an incredible success. To date, fourteen young mothers have fulfilled their educational dreams and secured subsequent meaningful full-time employment because of the generosity of Veronica and Durwood Hardy.

The other result of their generosity has been a total change in the way most of the Bouvier community feel about Durwood and Veronica. The business and social establishment have embraced them. Their church followers adore their leadership of the Bouvier Lutheran Church. And the rest of the community remains incredibly jealous and envious of the Hardys. But such is the case in most small towns throughout the country.

Dressed in a black button-up blouse, jeans, and with her hair pulled back, Veronica looked her usual elegant self that morning. In her mid fifties, most would guess her age to be the mid thirties. As soon as she sat down, Veronica could tell that the topic of Durwood and Mary's conversation was unpleasant.

"Ok, I can tell that the two of you need a change in your discussion topic. You both look very serious, and it appears that your topic is quite ominous. I think everyone here this morning is scared to death by your expressions." Veronica's levity was a welcome relief to their discussion. Durwood thought, "If Veronica only knew how right she was in her assessment." He also knew that she was only half kidding. If the patrons in Ruby's saw Durwood and Mary appearing to have a very serious and grim conversation, the rumor mills would begin to heat up to ascertain what they were talking about.

Mary and Durwood brightened up with Veronica's appearance. Durwood immediately got to the important topic of their breakfast orders. Veronica then made both Durwood and Mary feel guilty when she ordered the breakfast fruit plate.

Emerald playfully acted incredulous when Veronica placed her order. "Now, Miss Veronica, I will make sure the fruit plate is delicious for you. But do you have any idea what kind of real breakfast you are passing up? I mean, from what I have heard this morning from numerous customers, our pecan pancakes are to die for. Are you sure you don't want to come to your senses?"

Veronica laughed and politely declined Emerald's offer. She loved Emerald and the verbal back and forth that Emerald loved to play with her customers. After getting the important issue of her breakfast order out of the way, Mary asked her mom if she had any big plans for her day. Veronica stated that she would drop by the church for a little while after breakfast to meet with one of the women's groups as they prepared for a fall luncheon that would be held the next month. After that she was planning on taking Clare McMasters to lunch. Veronica elaborated that she sensed that Haley's death was taking a toll on Clare, since the two had been so close prior to Haley's death.

As soon as Veronica mentioned the lunch plans with Clare, she could sense something wasn't right with her daughter and husband. Both Mary and Durwood immediately buried their heads and focused on their amazing breakfast platters.

They acted as if they were famished and the sight of food was bringing them an inexplicable relief, but their routine wasn't working with Veronica. She smiled as Mary and Durwood avoided eye contact. The silence at their table was especially noticeable and very uncomfortable for Mary and Durwood. Veronica let the silence remain for several seconds, which seemed like minutes or even hours to the other two. Finally, she cruelly broke the verbal void by asking, "Would the two of you like to join Clare and me for lunch?" Upon hearing those words, Durwood almost chocked on one of the pecans that was nestled in his prized pancakes. He began to cough and turned slightly pink before dislodging the pecan. Before anything else could be said, Veronica responded to her own question, "I guess I should take that as a strong no."

Nothing else was needed to be said as Veronica completely understood that she was heading into potentially dangerous waters with her lunch date with Clare McMasters. But she also understood that she didn't want to know any details of what Durwood and Mary apparently had gleaned, because she wanted to be able to honestly talk with her friend without having to cover up some confidentially held information. Additionally, it would not place her in any compromising situation if Clare asked her if she knew anything about Haley's death. She did not and that was the way she wanted it to be. As they finished their delightful breakfast, Veronica's curiosity was in overdrive as she wondered what her beloved husband and daughter had uncovered. She took solace in the thought that whatever it was, it wouldn't remain a secret very long in the gossip mills that occupied the quaint town of Bouvier.

CHAPTER 11

THE REENACTMENT of the Civil War battle near Bouvier was scheduled for weekend following Haley's funeral. A Civil War fanatic, Mitch McMasters had become a regular on the local reenactment circuit. Even though he did not want to venture out in public, he knew that missing the weekend battle would be noticed by all of his acquaintances. In the meantime, he put in as little time at the newspaper as possible. Clare had prepared a moving memorial to Haley, which included written memories from a multitude of Haley's classmates and friends. Wanting to stay far away from the Haley issue, Mitch mailed in a lame editorial that week about the importance of grandparents in honor of Grandparents Day. As usual, the editorial ended up being a self serving way for Mitch to remind everyone in Barry County of all the important things his grandparents had done for the county. By the end of the editorial most readers could easily come to the conclusion that Barry County would not have existed without the tireless leadership and generosity of the McMasters family. Even though it was not his intent, Mitch later viewed the editorial as a prime weapon in his support if he ever got into any type of harms way resulting from Haley's death. His defense would be, don't mess with the McMasters family, because you owe us a break here and there in return for all that we have done for you free loaders.

It was a beautiful September day as the horde of Civil War reenactors converged upon Bouvier. Even though a true Civil War battle never took place inside the city limits of Bouvier, it didn't stop the ceremonial battle from taking place at the city's luscious park's complex. A wall of people milled around the complex. The various soldiers in their blue and gray uniforms give the event an authentic Civil War era look. The sight of snow cone, cotton candy, and funnel cake vendors scattered around the grounds clearly detracted from the venue. They also gave one pause as to whether the true Civil War battle could have been impacted by the surge of energy from having eaten one of Alma Boxley's famed funnel cakes.

Mitch McMasters arrived shortly before noon. The sight of the large crowd and the beautiful radiant sun brightened up his mood. As soon as he arrived, Mitch milled around talking with the fellow reenactors. As a proud member of the Confederate army, Mitch was scheduled to lead his group into battle at 1:00 pm. According to the plan, he would be valiantly shot and killed by a Union counterpart by 2:00 pm. This would give Mitch a couple of hours to get his mind off the matter of Haley's death and the continual stress and worry over whether anyone would ever look into the circumstances leading up to her passing. He had been in similar battle reenactments before, but Mitch loved the adrenaline that resulted from being in battle. At times he wished he had been born a hundred years earlier and had been given the opportunity to lead a true charge of Confederate soldiers into battle. But today he settled for a brave, symbolic fight and death in honor on the Confederate cause at the south end of the Bouvier city park at 1:55 pm, Central Daylight Time.

After lying dead for his prescribed time period, Mitch got up and started to leave the reenactment for the refuge of his lake cabin. Just as he was walking to his car, he bumped into Rufus Jones, a fellow reenactor. Jones specialized in buying and selling used cars, boats, horses, and mobile homes. He also did auto body work in his spare time. Rufus and his brother, Roscoe, dabbled in the marketing of stolen car parts when Roscoe wasn't serving time in the Barry County jail for various offenses against the fine citizens of Bouvier and the surrounding communities. Needless to say, Rufus Jones was not going to be seen at any Chamber of Commerce, Rotary Club, or Lutheran Church gatherings in Bouvier. Seeing Rufus was just what Mitch needed on this bright and gorgeous day.

After a round of small talk, Mitch invited Rufus down to the lake cabin. He said, "Rufus, come on down this evening to the cabin. We will go out on the lake, drink some beer, and talk about a project that I need your assistance." The offer of a boat ride and free beer wasn't anything Rufus would turn down, regardless of what he might have already had planned for the evening. Rufus was astute enough to know that when Mitch McMasters mentioned a "project" it meant, 'I need something done and done in a manner that nobody knows about it.' Rufus also knew that these types of jobs for Mitch paid very well due to his desired discretion. Rufus had handled some "projects" for Mitch before, and, so far, Mitch had never been burned by Rufus. He received his generous fee and kept his damn mouth shut. Rufus gladly accepted Mitch's offer and agreed to meet him at Mitch's dock at 7:00 p.m. By then the sun would be going down, and fewer people would be able to see him with Rufus.

Mitch smiled as he approached his car. It has been the first day since Haley had informed him that she was pregnant that things had gone well. There were several clouds hanging over him with regards to Haley's death; but if Rufus would accept his "project" assignment tonight, it would eliminate one of the biggest clouds. Mitch enjoyed his trip home as he listened to his favorite Willie Nelson songs on his iPod.

THE ONLY obstacles to a successful meeting with Rufus would be an appearance by Clare or the prospect of every liquor store in the lake area being sold out of Rufus' favorite beer, Miller genuine draft. Mitch loved Budweiser, but he would sacrifice his taste preference that evening to achieve solidarity with Rufus Jones. To Mitch's delight, Clare chose a movie outing with Veronica Hardy and a couple of other friends, and the Lakeside Package Store was adequately stocked with Rufus' Miller Genuine Draft. Mitch could sense the start of a good evening.

As expected Rufus showed up in his beat up 1998 model Ford F150 pickup, which was adorned with the applicable Confederate emblems and conservative mantras such as "Guns don't kill people, Pissed off people kill people." When Mitch saw the emblem he immediately thought of another potential bumper sticker for his Jeep Grand Cherokee, "Cars don't kill people, desperate, half-drunk, philandering, husbands kill people," but he quickly moved his mind to other more positive thoughts.

Rufus walked forward; and as soon as Mitch started to shake hands with him, he could clearly smell that Rufus had gotten a head start on the Miller Genuine Draft. This concerned Mitch, as a drunken Rufus would more than likely not be able to remember his assigned task the next day. But after a few minutes of small talk, Mitch discerned that Rufus wasn't drunk. He was just a little on the happy side, but clearly cognizant enough to remember to understand their conversation the following day. Dressed in a white sleeveless t-shirt, commonly known in Bouvier as a "wife beater shirt," blue jean cut offs, and a pair of old Nike white high tops, Rufus was ready for a boat ride. Mitch was adorned in a pair of fashionable salmon colored knee length shorts; a white polo short sleeve shirt; a pair of leather boat shoes; and his customary orange visor, which featured the emblem of a popular restaurant in Panama City Beach named Lobster Bob's. This was Mitch's custom attire when boating or spending time at the lake during the summer.

Once they were clearly away from any nearby boaters and after they had downed their first Genuine Draft, Mitch opened up the conversation of his "project" for Rufus. During the afternoon Mitch had carefully rehearsed the exact wording of why he needed Rufus' help. In no way did he want to unwittingly lead Rufus down the wrong path and connect his problem with Haley's wreck. Keeping his problem as vague as possible, he led Rufus to believe that he had been driving on one of the various curvy lake roads and had been distracted by a cell phone call, thus resulting in his Jeep crashing into an iron fence post. Mitch sheepishly admitted that he had consumed at least two Budweiser's and didn't want to draw the local cops to the scene. Plus, Clare had been furious with his propensity to drive home from the country club after having a couple of rounds with his buddies, so he could not let her know about the accident.

Rufus appeared to buy Mitch's story. Mitch figured that his carefully prepared story had either been persuasive and convincing; or Rufus had consumed enough beer that anything said to him at this point of the day would seem creditable. They discussed a few details; and then before reaching the dock, Mitch sternly reminded Rufus that he would pay a premium for secrecy. But if Rufus ever breached the trust he would never work for Mitch again. From his tone and his reputation, Rufus was convinced that Mitch meant every word. Rufus liked the generous fees paid by Mitch, and he also loved being in Mitch's circle as his secret "projects" guy. So there was no way he would rat out Mitch McMasters.

They got out of the boat, and Rufus cleaned up the empty beer cans. The entire ride had been a six beer affair, three for each. Both were feeling pretty good. They decided to get the Jeep moved while it was dark, when there would be little traffic on the highways at this time of the night. Mitch drove to Rufus' shop by taking a selected route, which kept them from having to drive through the middle of Bouvier and any scrutiny from the local police force. Rufus followed behind; and from Mitch's vantage point he was driving normally, without any noticeable swerving into the other lanes of traffic

Things were going well until Mitch saw red flashing lights in his rear view mirror. As he witnessed them he thought, "This is great; I'm half drunk and driving a partially wrecked vehicle. Let's see, the crimes of DWI and leaving the scene of the accident. No problem." But to his and Rufus' relief, it was just a first responder on his way to a fire at Happy Acres Mobile Home Park, located east of Bouvier. Mitch knew that he was home free at that point, because nothing like a house fire excited the local law enforcement community. Mitch knew that every deputy in the county would be flying down in their patrol cruisers to witness the mobile home fire. His wrecked Jeep would be the least of their worries and would definitely pale in comparison to a fire. As he suspected, they reached Rufus' fine establishment without incident. Rufus opened the door to his back garage and Mitch parked it in the open spot in the middle section. Rufus and Mitch carefully covered it with a blue tarp.

After walking outside, Mitch observed the level of the weeds growing around the two garages at Rufus' place and Mitch thought, "Hell, why cover the Jeep with a tarp; we could park in Rufus' weed patch and no one would find it until the first hard frost in late October."

The drive back to Mitch's cabin was an experience in itself. Rufus' old Ford F150 truck was filled with cat hair. Apparently, Rufus was a cat lover because there was enough cat hair in the cab of his truck to produce the world's largest hair ball. And to make matters worse, the beer was really starting to hit Rufus. As he came upon the Kit Kat Bar, a rough cowboy establishment located outside of Bouvier, Rufus made a plea to stop for another round of beer. Mitch was able to discourage Rufus from the Kit Kat Bar. Mitch kept thinking: "Just get me home without a wreck, an arrest, or a severe allergy attack from the cat hair, and the evening can be declared an overwhelming success."

Rufus courageously drove past two more bars, and Mitch could see the home stretch for the lake cabin. But just at the moment that he was beginning to feel a sense of ease, they saw bright flashing lights. The mobile home fire had caused a nearby propane tank to catch on fire and explode. The police and sheriff's department had closed the nearby roads as they dealt with a horrible mess of four mobile homes being charred as a result of the explosion. This caused their trip back to the cabin to take another forty-five minutes, a time period in which Mitch swore he heard Rufus begin to snore on more than one occasion as he was attempting to drive on the curvy lake roads. Finally, they safely arrived back at Mitch's cabin at 1:15 a.m.

Concerned with Rufus' ability to drive home, Mitch asked him to come in and sleep off the beer in the guest room. Rufus declined, but before he could turn on the ignition to his truck, he fell over on the passenger seat. Within two minutes Mitch could hear Rufus snoring loud enough to wake his golden retriever, Pete. Rufus slept in the truck until 5:00 a.m. when a crow landed on the hood of the truck and began to squawk loud enough to awaken the drunken Rufus Jones. By this time Mitch was resting comfortably inside the cabin. It was the first restful night in over two weeks. He had a sense that his potential troubles were about to become things of the past.

CHAPTER 12

AFTER A WEEK of gathering evidence, reports, and conducting preliminary interviews, on a beautiful Monday morning in September, Sheriff Buford Blakeley was ready to meet with Ernie Lambert to discuss where they were and where they should go in the investigation of Haley Fulz' fatal car crash. Buford was in his office wrapping up a review of the criminal warrants that had been issued and the fire caused by an explosion of a meth lab at the Happy Ackers Mobile Home Park from the previous weekend when he received a call from Durwood Hardy, a call that he sensed would help clear up many of the questions that were swirling in his mind regarding Haley's death. The news from Durwood was simple: a teenage girl from their church youth group had some valuable information regarding Haley. Durwood couldn't discuss the other two girls' information without their consent.

Durwood's call clearly piqued Buford's interest. He quickly got with Ernie Lambert and arranged a meeting time for that afternoon. After confirming things with Durwood, their next order of business was to meet with a crash scene investigator from the Missouri State Police. The investigator was a condescending nerd named Phillip Bottorfman, who did nothing but exam car crash sites. He was also one of the most boring speakers that Ernie or Buford had ever encountered, but he was also one of the leading experts in crash investigations in the Midwest. Dressed in a short sleeve blue dress shirt, wrinkled black slacks, black horn rimmed glasses, and a red bow tie, Mr. Bottorfman methodically reviewed his investigation of the Haley Fulz vehicle crash scene.

Mr. Bottorfman had taken more photos than Ernie or Buford could ever image and had even crawled down the mountain where Haley's car eventually landed. More photos were taken and shown of the landing spot for Haley's car. He had gone to the salvage yard where Haley's car was impounded and had taken a large volume of photos of the car. No one would ever be able of accusing Mr. Bottorfman of being sloppy in his work. He was one of the most meticulous people in his profession. After thirty-five minutes of excruciating details, Mr. Bottorfman uttered the magical words for Ernie and Buford's ears, "In conclusion, I, Phillip K. Bottorfman, special crash scene investigator for the Missouri State Police, conclude that the fatal wreck of Haley Fulz was the result of Ms. Fulz auto being struck from behind. It appears that Ms. Fulz overreacted after being struck by the auto, incorrectly swerved her vehicle, which caused it to become airborne and then crash on the hillside mountain. It was a horrific crash. It appears that the violent nature of the crash would most certainly have killed Ms. Fulz upon impact."

Buford was taken aback by how correct his initial assumption about the wreck turned out to be. Before Mr. Bottorfman could start another monotone sentence, Ernie Lambert interjected a question. "Mr. Bottorfman, tell us about what you know about the car that struck Haley's car?"

Without hesitation, Mr. Bottorfman stated, "Miss Fulz car was struck from behind by a black 2008 model Jeep Grand Cherokee." Before he could catch himself, Ernie flippantly asked, "Could you be a little more specific?"

The attempt at humor was clearly lost on Phillip K. Bottorfman, who appeared to be offended by the question. "Mr. Lambert, I challenge you to find someone who can bring you more specificity to the facts of this investigation. I have spent the past..."

Sensing that he had hurt Mr. Bottorfman's feelings with his poor attempt at humor, Lambert interjected, "Listen, Phillip, I was just joking. My joke was more of a compliment to your work than anything else. Buford and I are blown away by the thorough nature of your findings."

Buford chimed in, "Yeah, I agree with Ernie. You have worked your ass off on this case, Phil. You have done one hell of a job. I sure as hell couldn't have put things together like you did."

Mr. Bottorfman appeared to understand their affirmation for his work. But he was still peeved and condescending of their attitudes. Despite his hurt feelings, he continued on, "Gentleman, with the technological advances, our laboratory equipment can render a paint chip down to not only the type of vehicle, but also the exact year. At this point this technology works only for cars manufactured since 2004. We don't like to advertise this, because it reeks of big-brother; but within the next five years we will be able to track a paint chip back to a specific car. From there we will be able to trace it from the original owner on down to the current owner, as long as they have the vehicle registered with a state within the United States."

Buford and Ernie sat there stunned by Mr. Bottorfman's presentation. They were afraid to ask any additional questions for fear of hurting his feelings again. But Ernie couldn't let Mr. Bottorfman leave without sewing up some details.

"So Mr. Bottorfman, everything you have used to test the paint chip has been certified to stand up in the courts in Missouri. We are using some new experimental technology, are we?"

In his nasal voice, Mr. Bottorfman responded, "Mr. Lambert, you will find that the State Police has had the analyzer certified with the Supreme Court of the State of Missouri. The court issued their certification of the latest technology being used by the State Police on May 24, 2007. However, I caution both of you not to discuss the potential future advances that are just around the corner for our department. Not all find them appealing, especially, the civil liberties groups, if you know what I mean."

Buford was in awe and a bit scared of Mr. Bottorfman at this point. He was thinking, "I'm glad he's on our side. But what else does he have up there in Jeff City that he could use to spy on us?"

Before he concluded, he stated that while examining the mountainside crash site, he had found one additional item. At that moment he tossed to Ernie a sealed plastic bag which contained a cell phone and stated, "I bet this is Ms. Fulz cell phone. Maybe this will help your investigation." With that stunning conclusion, Mr. Phillip K. Bottorfman excused himself from the office of Ernie Lambert, Prosecuting Attorney for Barry County.

BEFORE THEY COULD catch their breath from their riveting meeting with Mr. Phillip K. Bottorfman, Ernie Lambert and Buford Blakeley were sitting down with Mary Hardy, Durwood Hardy, Lizzie Nicholas, and Lizzie's mom, Natalie Nicholas. Ernie looked around the room in his office and thought; "This is not going to be good, a young girl getting ready to discuss the last conversation with her dead best friend."

Ernie offered everyone water, coffee, and soft drinks. After all parties were properly hydrated, Ernie explained the purpose of the meeting and thanked all parties for taking the time out of their busy schedules to meet with him and Buford on this beautiful September day in the Ozarks. Mary discussed why they had come to the meeting. She elaborated that the information initially communicated by Lizzie had been in a confidential Pastor-Parishioner setting. By coming forward, Lizzie clearly understood that they were moving from a confidential setting and that the information she would give could be shared with law enforcement agencies if an investigation was opened into Haley's accident. Ernie asked Lizzie a few questions to make sure she clearly understood the type of setting she was now in, versus the church setting when she first discussed the matter with Mary Hardy. Lizzie and her mother were firm in their intent to discuss what she had learned from Haley.

Ernie asked Lizzie to tell what she had learned from Haley prior to her death. As she spoke, he and Buford focused just as much on her mannerisms as what she was saying. They wanted to see if various emotional points would come out in her talk. Was she confident in what she was saying? Did she appear to be angry? Was she fidgeting or overly anxious or nervous? Did she appear to have an agenda? Was she sincere? The more Lizzie spoke, the more Buford and Ernie became convinced that Lizzie was simply a young girl telling the truth about her beloved friend, who was now dead. Ernie and Buford each followed up on Lizzie's description of what Haley had told her with a few minor questions. Ernie asked Lizzie if she had told anyone other than the people in this room or the two girls, Kate Johnston and Morgan Langley. Lizzie confidently stated that she had not told anyone else. Then she added, "But I can't vouch for what Kate or Morgan may have said, since they were in the room when I told Mary. I don't think Morgan would tell anyone, but Kate is another story."

Ernie nodded in agreement, and then he asked, "So no one has offered you money to keep quiet or tried to intimidate you into keeping quiet about what you learned from Haley?"

Ernie's question caught everyone but Buford off guard, especially Lizzie and her mom. Lizzie's mother's face was bright red and her eyes gave the impression that she was upset. Before Lizzie could answer, her mom started to talk, "Mr. Lambert, are we in danger for coming forward? Your question really concerns me."

Ernie coolly deflected the reply by recapping what Lizzie had communicated: specifically, that Haley was pregnant because she was having an affair with a married guy, who happened to be very successful and influential. "And Mrs. Nicholas, you are surprised that this person might want this information to go away. No, you are not in danger. But if anyone contacts you, you get with us immediately. That's how witnesses stay out of danger."

Lizzie confidently broke the silence, "I have not been contacted by anyone. Nor has my mom. And I will not be bought. My dignity is not for sale, thank you."

A smiling Ernie Lambert stepped closer to Lizzie and said, "I knew the answer before I asked the question; I just wanted to hear it from you. We appreciate you coming here today. I know it isn't easy. I can tell that Haley was a wonderful friend, and you will always love her. I am very proud of you, and I know your mom is as well." Ernie's remarks and his confident presence clearly made a positive impression with Lizzie and her mom. He asked the question for a reason, but he also wanted them to understand that he meant business, and the other party involved with Haley would mean business as well. But his objective to determine Lizzie's resolve and the validity of her story was a success. Ernie asked Lizzie and her mom if they had anything else they wanted to add.

At this point Natalie Nicholas looked Ernie Lambert straight in the eye with a laser beam type presence and pointed her finger, "Let me back up what Lizzie just said. No one, not even Mitch McMasters or the McMasters family, can buy our dignity or our self respect. Do you understand me?"

Natalie Nicholas comment sucked all the air out of the room. She had the guts to utter what all parties in the room had been quietly wondering, "Was Haley messing around with Mitch McMasters?"

Ernie Lambert knew he had to inquire further with Natalie Nicholas as to why Mitch McMasters had come up in the conversation; but at the same time, he didn't want things to get out of hand. "Ok, time out here, Natalie; where did the Mitch McMasters thing come from? Tell me why you brought up Mitch McMasters in this matter?"

"Mr. Lambert, I talked to Olivia Langley, Morgan Langley's mom. You know Kate Johnston's parents won't let her talk to you, but I think Chase and Olivia Langley will let Morgan discuss what she saw with Haley and Mitch."

"Ok, Natalie, what you know right now is second hand information, isn't it?

The cute little spunky Natalie Nicholas was not about to be sidetracked or swayed from telling what she knew. "Mr. Lambert, I don't care what you call it. I would call it pointing you and Buford in the right direction. That's what I would call it. You know the old saying, 'You can lead a horse to water, but you can't make him drink.' Well, consider what I am doing as leading you and Buford to water. If you don't drink, that is your fault, not mine. But mind you, I will be very determined in seeing that you do drink the water."

Ernie and Buford were clearly enjoying the feisty Mrs. Nicholas. Ernie replied, "I really appreciate where you are coming from. If Morgan or Kate will voluntarily come forward, it will help clear up the water that Buford and I are trying to drink. And it will make it more appealing for others to drink, if you know what I mean, Natalie."

"I most certainly do. I clearly understand where you are coming from. But until they do come forward, I would suggest that you take a serious look at Mitch McMasters. Because from what Olivia Langley has told me, Haley and Mitch were up to no good this summer. She said Morgan and Kate saw the two of them passionately kissing and rubbing around on each other. You take what they saw, combined with what Haley told Lizzie, and it adds up to Mitch McMasters."

"Natalie, I appreciate your assistance, I really do. I just want to make sure we aren't taking two plus two and coming up with sixty-four."

"So does that mean you aren't going to do anything because it involves Mitch McMasters?"

"No, that is not what I meant. I will treat this just like any case regardless of who is involved. I will follow the evidence, plain and simple. I need evidence, not hearsay. But you cannot go around town saying Mitch McMasters is involved. You do that and then this investigation will go south real quick. I have seen investigations go to hell real fast when people start shooting off their mouth. You let me and Buford handle the investigation and the way in which we communicate the investigation. Do you understand?"

"I sure do. I will keep my big mouth shut until you tell me otherwise. But you better take what I told you seriously. Do you understand me?"

"You know, Natalie, I think we are both crystal clear in our understanding of each other's intended communication." With that they both shared a good laugh and the tension in the room was lifted.

Ernie and Buford thanked everyone for coming to the meeting. As he was leaving, Durwood Hardy gave Ernie a look that said, "Boy, you are in the big game; and they throw hard ball in this league." Durwood gently whispered to Ernie, "Call me any time you need someone to talk to. This is going to be tough. We both know it. But you can do it"

After everyone had left, Ernie and Buford sat down and discussed their next moves. A case that they had suspected would end up going nowhere had changed suddenly in the matter of three hours. Now, they were potentially going to be going after the most powerful man in the county in a case that, if proven to be true, will sicken and revolt most of the God fearing people in Bouvier. The thought of a father impregnating his son's girlfriend was sickening. For it to be someone from the county's most renowned family would be even more shocking.

Two hours later they wrapped things up and had their game plan in place for the remainder of the week. They both chuckled at the thought of Mitch McMasters sitting back having a cold one either on the golf course or on one of his boats totally oblivious to the fact that he had just had a really bad day without even knowing about it.

Ernie Lambert arrived home after six o'clock that evening. His wife, Sherlene, could immediately tell he had had a really good day. After helping his kids with their home work, Ernie snuck into his den where he prepared notes on his laptop for the days to come. He had the case he had always dreamed of, and he couldn't wait to pursue it with full vengeance. After the kids were asleep, Ernie and Sherlene snuggled under the bedroom sheets and had a passionate end to a full day. That Monday in September was truly a good day for Ernie Lambert. He slept like a baby. At the other end of town, for some strange reason Mitch McMasters had a fitful night's rest.

CHAPTER 13

THE TIMING of the press release from his office had been carefully calculated. After conversing with the Fulz family, Buford Blakeley's secretary emailed it to the *Bouvier Gazette* within ninety minutes of their deadline for the week. Ernie Lambert and Buford Blakeley wanted it exactly that way. It would make the paper, but Clare McMasters wouldn't have time to reach Buford or Ernie for a comment. That would allow them some additional time before they would have to talk publicly about the case. Additionally, it would give them time to smoke out Mitch McMasters. Would he hold up under their pressure, start to fold, or lash out from his editorial page? The timing also meant Mitch would have to wait a week before he could get anything in print that would paint Buford or Ernie in a bad light. They expected the worst. But they also hoped to get Mitch rattled. Only time would tell.

Clare McMasters had just arrived back from lunch. She had discussed the placement of two photos for the *Gazette's* sports section with her sports editor and was finishing up her article on the meth lab explosion at the Happy Acres Mobile Home Park when at 1:30 p.m. an email showed up on her computer from the office of Sheriff Buford Blakeley. The subject line of the email immediately caught her attention. It simply said: Haley Fulz Crash Investigation Update. When Clare saw the email she couldn't open up the item fast enough. Clare was not happy at the sight of the email; and as a result, the first thing that ran through her mind as she was opening the email was, "What investigation? When, who, and why had someone launched an investigation; and why hadn't she been alerted?" Clare opened and read the following:

Sheriff Buford Blakeley is asking the public for assistance in the investigation of the fatal car crash, which took the life of Haley Fulz. The wreck took place at approximately 11:00 pm on Tuesday, September 4. Anyone who may have witnessed the accident or who may have witnessed another car leave the scene of the wreck should immediately contact Sheriff Blakeley. Blakeley stated, "We need the public's assistance in finding the identity of a mystery vehicle that may have been involved in the accident. Specifically, we are looking for a black Jeep Grand Cherokee. At this time we cannot state if the other vehicle was intentionally or unintentionally involved or whether foul play was involved. This case is a top priority for the Barry County Sheriff's department. I have instructed my officers to use their full diligence in this matter. Your assistance is greatly appreciated." Sheriff Buford Blakeley, Barry County Sheriff

Once the email had been sent, Buford left his office and told his secretary that he was not to be disturbed for the next two hours, especially if Clare McMasters called. His secretary, Sammie Burger, chuckled at Buford's comments, as she knew exactly what Buford meant. In less than two minutes after Buford had spoken those words, Sammie Burger answered the phone only to hear the voice of Clare McMasters. Sammie thought she was prepared for her mission, but she had no idea what she was about to encounter on the other end of the phone. Clare was not about to accept some jive from Buford's secretary.

"What do you mean the Sheriff is not available? He just prepared an email, which he sent to me. So I find it terribly hard to believe that he is suddenly unavailable. Let's try this again, Sammy. Where is Buford? Sammy, I know you know; and I know you are covering for our sweet little friend at this moment."

A visibly rattled Sammie Burger didn't know what to say. Talking to Clare McMasters scared the hell out of her. But ratting out Buford and potentially losing her job also scared her equally well. Sammy took a deep breath and said, "Miss Clare I am sorry, but Buford gave me specific instructions that he was not to be disturbed this afternoon. He said it was important. Do you want me to get fired?"

"Sammy, I am not trying to be difficult, but I have a job to do and you are interfering with it. So if there is an emergency in the county in the next hour, you are saying Buford isn't going respond?"

"I just said the Sheriff isn't available at this time."

"Ok, is he available right now to the boys at Ruby's or is he available at the moment to Ernie Lambert? And if you lie to me, I will publish this very conversation in this week's edition of the Gazette. I'm sure Buford would love to have this story on the front page."

A weakened Sammy Burger couldn't take any more bullying from Clare McMasters. The thought of becoming part of a news story was something she wanted to avoid at all costs. Sammy blurted out, "Well, Miss Clare, I'm pretty sure he's not at Ruby's."

An agitated and condescending Clare concluded, "Thank you, Sammy, you've been quite helpful." She immediately hung up and headed for Ernie Lambert's office.

Sammy Burger sat at her desk for several minutes unable to move. She worried about what Buford was about to encounter from Clare; more importantly, she also worried if she would have a job the next day.

CLARE McMASTERS arrived at Ernie Lambert's office within five minutes after her terse exchange with Sammie Burger. Dressed in a very becoming summer weight khaki skirt, which ran below her knees, and a stylish blue blouse, Clare was as elegant looking as ever. Ernie's receptionist, a tough long-time courthouse employee named Blanche Murtrey, was ready for Clare. Sammie had done one thing right: she called Ernie's office and gave them a partially true story of her encounter with Clare McMasters. The only portion of Sammie's story that was true was the part about Clare coming their way. Clare arrived hot and out of breath at the second floor office. She demanded to see Buford Blakeley and Ernie Lambert. Blanche looked at Clare with her glasses perched at the end of her nose and rudely said, "They are in a meeting and are not to be disturbed."

A clearly perturbed Clare was in no mood for any lip from Blanche Murtrey. She looked at her and said, "Unless they are meeting with the Governor, Attorney General, or Judge Claibourn, I strongly suggest they squeeze in a little time in their busy schedules to see me."

Blanche was not about to be intimidated. She looked up at Clare and tersely said, "Have a seat."

Clare glared at Blanche's wrinkled forehead for several moments, and Blanche glared right back. Clare finally blinked and arrogantly said, "What do you mean have a seat? I am not leaving until I talk to Ernie and Buford."

Blanche didn't respond. She stared right back at Clare in a manner that said, "Don't mess with me, prissy lady. Blanche then stood up from her chair and took a slow walk to the back of the office. She didn't glance back, because she knew Clare didn't have the guts to defy her. It was her turf, and Clare knew it, even if she was putting up a strong front.

Blanche arrived back to her desk within a couple of minutes and coolly informed Clare that Ernie and Buford would be with her in a few minutes. Clare was not happy with the response. She stood up and informed Blanche that she was working under a deadline, and she needed to speak Ernie and Buford immediately.

Blanche barely glanced up when she said, "They know you are here, and they know you are being very impatient and that you are pissed off. There isn't much more I can do. Do you still want to wait?"

Clare wasn't about to take some grief from Blanche. "Are you always this rude? I sincerely hope you aren't this rude with people who come into this office, a tax payer funded office for your information on a daily basis."

"Clare, are you always this way or are you just having a really bad day?"

As soon as she heard Blanche's question Clare's eyes began to moisten. The tough girl showdown was over. The emotions of everything in her life had hit a boiling point, and Clare simply sat in the chair and began to sob. The war with Blanche Murtrey was officially over when Blanche offered Clare a tissue for her tears.

Ernie Lambert called for Clare to come back to his office after making her cool her heels for over nine minutes. It was a seldom used tactic for Ernie. But he was really ticked off at Clare for her high-handed manner that afternoon. Ernie decided to go on the offensive before Clare could bombard him and Buford with questions.

"Clare, you and I have been working together for a long, long time. I have never seen you act this way. What the hell is wrong with you? This isn't New York, Washington, or St. Louis. Damn, Clare, this is Bouvier and where do you get off acting like some Yankee reporter?"

"Where do you and Buford get off dumping an important press release on me right at my deadline? I deserve better, and you know it. And don't give me any Yankee crap, Ernie. That isn't going to work with me today."

"When did we start coordinating our press releases with your deadlines, Clare? Why are you so upset?"

With tears rolling down her face, Clare cleared the air. "You know why I'm upset. Haley was like a daughter to me. For Christ sakes, she was dating my son; we bought her the car she died in, and she worked for me at the *Gazette* all summer. You knew all this guys. So why didn't you call me up and tell me what was going on? Instead, you send me a carefully worded email. Normally you call me up and say, 'Hey Clare, here is what we can say about the blah, blah, blah case.' But no you couldn't. So what's going on?"

"You are exactly right, Clare. This is different. We have a very popular and beloved seventeen year old die inexplicably in a horrific car wreck. We have to get this one right. So we wanted our press release to be as precise as possible. You weren't the only press outlet to get it. We are not going to be sloppy. We are getting this right. So speaking of getting it right, you hear everything going around town, what is being said about Haley's wreck?"

"Ernie, I have been so despondent about what has happened, to be honest, I have been keeping to myself lately. I honestly don't know what is being said. I'm sure the usual tongues are wagging, especially since we were connected to Haley."

"What is Mitch hearing? He's usually out and about?" Ernie asked the question about Mitch to see if he could get a reaction from Clare. As expected the question seemed to affect Clare.

"Mitch has been busy with his fishing and golfing. He hasn't been at the paper very much lately. But thanks for asking." Ernie and Buford could tell that she was pissed about the Mitch question. She paused, started to say something else, but withdrew.

Ernie decided to continue his line of questions for Clare, "How bad are you going to rip us? Do Buford and I need to start having fundraisers for our re-election bids?"

"Ernie, I expected better from you. Is re-election all you guys think about?"

"If it were, I wouldn't be pursuing this case," responded Ernie.

"And what does that mean, Ernie?"

"You will see, sooner or later. And you will understand what I mean at that time."

Clare, visibly upset, immediately left Ernie's office. She had not achieved anything she had set out to do. And she had left with more unanswered questions than when she had arrived.

Clare rushed to the newspaper office and hurriedly finished the week's edition. As she continued to work, she kept going back to Ernie's question about what Mitch had heard about Haley's wreck. Ernie and Mitch had never been close. In fact, she had never seen Ernie ask about Mitch. The thought kept going through her mind, "Does Mitch know something about the wreck that he hasn't shared." After several more minutes of work, Clare decided to call Chad, who was back to school in Columbia, to let him know about the press release that Buford had issued. She didn't want him to be surprised when he received the issue of the *Gazette* at school. The phone call with Chad did not go well. Clare found him to be distant and somewhat unconcerned with her news. She was shocked by his reaction. Clare was thinking that something else had to be wrong. So being the concerned mom that she was, Clare pried for more information. But Chad continued to deflect her questions. He was ok, school was ok, and everything was fine with the frat. But he seemed totally unconcerned with the investigation of Haley's wreck. Finally, Clare hit the raw nerve that had triggered Chad's demeanor.

"Listen, Mom, I don't want to hear about Haley anymore. Do you understand me?"

"Chad, I do understand. I know it hurts. I hurt everyday. But sometimes it helps to talk about these things. I'm afraid that retreating and not discussing your hurt and your feelings will be harmful for you. I know talking about Haley can hurt, but expressing your hurt and your pain can also be a positive release for you mentally."

"Ok, Mom, you want release, here's my release and expression of my hurt. She used and embarrassed us. I have found out that while I was in Italy, she was messing around with one or possibly two people."

"What, she was at the paper everyday. And she worked late several evenings. Are you sure some girls aren't trying to get to you by planting these kinds of stories about Haley?"

"Mom, you don't understand, I have heard this from some pretty straight shooting people. And get this Mom; Haley was pregnant when she died. And I can assure you, it wasn't my kid."

"Chad, where did you here this? Are you sure?"

"Mom, I am sure on both accounts. She was pregnant, and it wasn't mime. I was gone for nearly four months by the time Haley died. I heard she found out she was pregnant right before she died."

"This can't be, Chad. I really think you have been fed some bad information. I really do."

"No, Mom; I am right. You will find out sooner or later. So not to be rude, but don't call me with any additional Haley updates. I don't care anymore. She's dead to me in more than just one way. She just used me to get that car and probably the job. That's all she was." Chad began to breakdown as Clare could hear the sobs on the other end of the phone. Despite the strong front, Chad was as hurt as anyone over Haley's death. He had loved her and then to find out that he had been betrayed was more than he could take at the moment. Clare decided to let him use his indifference as his defense mechanism, at the moment. But she would stay in close touch. Because she had seen and heard of too many situations where the hurt and embarrassed party end up doing something rash when they are encountering deep emotional hurt and pain.

Clare concluded her call by telling Chad she loved him and she would abide by his wishes. Chad strengthened as their call concluded and told his mom that he appreciated her concern and that he loved her as well. After she hung up, Clare was in a daze for several moments. What Chad had told her had totally thrown her off balance mentally and emotionally. After reflecting on the call for several minutes, she also realized that

Chad hadn't even mentioned his father's name once. The last few hours of her day had been terrible, and Clare was drained emotionally.

Ernie Lambert's inquiry about Mitch continued to bug Clare. This prompted her to give her husband a call to let him know about the press release issued and to let him know about Chad's emotional state and what he had told her about Haley. If Mitch had heard something about the wreck, Clare felt that she would be able to sense it very quickly. She was confident that Mitch didn't know about the pregnancy. She knew that he would have called her immediately if he had heard any such news. Little did she know what had taken place between Haley and Mitch. But the main reason she called was to just have someone to vent to at a time when she felt like her world was spinning around her at a speed much faster than she could absorb.

Haley's death had been a terrific blow to Clare. To find out in a matter of three hours that her death was now being investigated as a suspicious act and that her beloved son believed Haley was pregnant at the time of her death with someone else's child added more to her emotional plate than she could handle at the moment. Her emotional pity party came to a crashing halt when she thought of Jackie Fulz and what she was going through. Clare immediately wondered if Jackie knew about the pregnancy. She wanted to call Jackie; but at the same time, she didn't want to appear to be prying for information. So she reached for her cell phone and called Mitch instead.

CLARE reached Mitch on the second ring of his prized new cell phone. Always trying to impress, Mitch would grab up the latest technology enhancements, whether it was cell phones, personal planners, travel equipment, or music gadgets. Mitch's smart phone was now five months old, but he still treasured it as is it were a new friend. Mitch was in the parking lot of the Bouvier Country Club after a tough day on the links when Clare reached him. Since their communication had been limited of late, Mitch was surprised to hear from his wife. As soon as he answered, he could sense that things were not good with Clare. After a brief exchange of how their days had gone, Clare got right to the point.

"Have you heard anything about Haley's wreck? Is there anything being talked around town or at the club about the wreck?"

Mitch paused, took a deep breath, and told himself to act a casual as possible and ask lots of questions without sounding defensive.

"No, other than people continuing to come up and express their sympathy for the loss. Have you heard something?"

"Nothing until about three hours ago. And in that time period, I have been blown away by what I have heard."

A nervous Mitch didn't know what to say. Had Clare discovered the real story? He once again breathed deeply and tried to act as casual as possible.

"So Clare, what has happened in the last few hours that has you so upset?"

"Well, first the Sheriff dumps a carefully worded press release on me right at my deadline, which says that they are investigating her wreck and are looking for a suspicious vehicle that may have been at the scene of her wreck."

Mitch absorbed this without peeing his pants, but it wasn't easy.

Then Clare continued, "The next thing I learn from my call to Chad is that Haley was supposedly pregnant when she died.

Chad is devastated at the thought of Haley secretly having a sexual relationship with someone while he was in Italy. It is horrible. He hates Haley now. The girl he was in love with is now the person he despises the most in the world. And he can never talk to her about what happened or to hear from her if any of this is true because she is dead. I just want to hold our baby so bad. But he is hurt and I can tell he is going to respond by putting up an emotional wall to deal with his pain. I don't want him to become a hardened uncaring person because of this. You know that happens sometimes to people who have been hurt and who respond to the hurt by shutting down their emotions. Other than that, my day has just been grand. Oh, to top it all off, I was so upset about the press release, I made a fool of myself with both Buford's and Ernie's receptionists. I feel so horrible. My nerves have been raw since Haley died, and the press release just hit one of the raw ones."

Mitch immediately thought, "Well, hell Clare, your day is a picnic compared to what I have just heard. They are looking for me at the scene of the crime, and someone knew she was pregnant. This is just grand!"

Mitch carefully responded back to Clare. "Clare, I don't know what to say. I can't imagine what you were feeling when you heard both sets of news. Did the Sheriff tell you anything about what they are looking for or what they know about the wreck?"

"I don't know; I'm too drained to remember. All it really says is they are looking for a black Jeep Grand Cherokee." When Mitch heard those words his heart began to race like a thoroughbred's as it's coming down the finish line. For a moment Mitch thought he was actually about to have a heart attack. He couldn't speak because he couldn't catch his breath. Clare heard something to startle her; and she called out, "Mitch are you ok. You are breathing really heavy. Are you ok?"

He finally regained his composure, or, at least he hoped he had, and responded, "Yeah, I'm ok. I'm just walking to the car. Man is it hot today. How about I come by and look at what they put out. Have you had dinner?"

"No, I'm so drained I lost my appetite several hours ago."

"Are you sure? We could run down to Castle Rock and get a steak at Charlie's."

"Mitch, thanks, but I'm going home and curling up on the sofa. With what has transpired, I feel like crying the night away."

Mitch accepted Clare's dinner decision in stride. He said that he would probably drop by the paper and work on an editorial for the next week and would be home after that. Before he could hang up, Clare added, "One more thing Mitch, would you call Chad before you head home? He's really down, and I think it would help if you would talk him through this." Before Mitch could answer, Clare concluded by asking, "When I was meeting or screaming at Ernie and Buford, however you would describe our get together, Ernie asked if I would go after them in the paper, because I was so upset over the press release. In fact, he asked if and Buford needed to start their fundraising efforts for the re-election campaigns. I then said something like, is getting re-elected all you guys think about? His response was, 'If it were, I wouldn't be pursuing this case.' His response struck me as odd, so I asked Ernie what he meant, and he said, 'You will see, sooner or later. And you will understand what I mean, at that time.' Is it just me, or is that strange? Do you have any idea where he's coming from on this? I'm too tired to think it through right now."

A terrified Mitch McMasters stood with his cell phone stuck to his ear, unsure how to respond. He felt like he was being hunted by Ernie Lambert. He finally collected himself to respond, "Yeah, uh, yeah, I'm like you; I'm too worn out to figure out what Ernie was saying. With Ernie, who knows. I've never understood half the stuff he says sometimes. You know all that prosecutor bull shit he likes to use. I'll see you at home."

Mitch immediately jumped into his car and sped to the offices of the *Bouvier Gazette* as fast as he could. In a few minutes the edition would be going to press, and Mitch knew he had to beat the deadline. This was the most important deadline in his journalistic career. His life as a free man was potentially on the line with this one.

The next morning the residents of Bouvier and all of Barry County would read about the Sheriff's investigation into Haley Fulz wreck in the *Bouvier Gazette*. Included in the front page article would be the press release from Sheriff Buford Blakeley, except for one missing item. There would be no mention of a black Jeep Grand Cherokee in the article. Mitch McMasters was able to meet, quite possibly the most important deadline of his career at the *Bouvier Gazette*. Time would only tell if it would save or merely delay his fate as the man who murdered Haley Fulz.

CHAPTER 14

MITCH McMASTERS awoke early the next morning, showered, and was out of the McMasters elegant residence before five o'clock. Clare had fallen asleep on the sofa in their den and had slept there the entire night. She was still sleeping soundly when Mitch drove down their magnolia-lined lane to head into town. He had slept maybe two or three hours max as he had so many things going through his mind. He was caught so off guard by the apparent knowledge of the wreck by Buford Blakeley that he didn't know where to turn.

He headed straight to Rufus Jones' place and woke him from his nightly beer coma. Luckily for Mitch, Rufus had finished the repairs on the Jeep Grand Cherokee. Since it was still dark, they decided it was an opportune time to transport it back to Mitch's place. They took all of the necessary back roads and had it safely parked in Mitch's garage before the sun came up. Mitch repeatedly inspected the work and was pleasantly surprised by the excellent work Rufus had performed. He was confident that no one would detect that the vehicle had been wrecked. This made Mitch breathe a little easier, but he knew that he was still in a world of trouble. The press release made him realize that Buford knew way more than he should. Mitch had greatly underestimated Buford's investigative skills. As he had done the night before, he continued a game of what if. A game that was making him crazy, but it was hard for him to think about anything else. The eerie question that kept racing in Mitch's mind was, "What else do they know?"

The trip back to Rufus' house didn't help Mitch's mind set. In fact, it made it worse. Mitch explained to Rufus that he needed to vouch for his whereabouts on the evening of September 4.

"If anyone asks, tell them we were fishing and drinking beer until the wee hours that night."

Even though he rarely read the local paper, Rufus was suspicious of covering for Mitch, especially due to the way Mitch was acting. Rufus, however, also saw this as a golden business opportunity. Dressed in a dirty Tony Stewart T-shirt, worn jeans, and and pair of sandals, Rufus looked even rougher than normal. His breath was to the point of nauseating Mitch; the aroma of the previous night's Genuine Draft filled the air in Mitch's car. Rufus leaned forward, pointed his finger at Mitch and said, "What the hell are you getting me into here, Mitch? It sounds like I'm getting myself in kind of deep. What's this worth to you?"

"What are you talking about, Rufus? There is nothing wrong; I just need a little cover. A man needs to be a man sometimes, and sometimes things need to be kept secret."

"So this is over a girl? That's all it is?"

"Well, sort of. But like I said, it is nothing serious. So save me the shake down because it's not going to happen."

"Ok, no problem. The deputies said they might be back later to ask some more questions. So if it's no big deal, I guess I don't need to tell them I was with you then." Not known for his subtlety, Rufus did a long stare to see if he had hit his intended mark with Mitch.

Mitch's pale white face combined with a slight quiver of his hands and lip tacitly answered Rufus' question.

Trying to act cool and collected, Mitch paused before he replied. "So Rufus, what's this Deputy Bull shit all about?"

"Listen Mitch, no bull shit. Yesterday, two of Buford's boys came by and asked some questions."

"Who came by and what did they ask? You sure you're not shitting me Rufus?"

"Sorry, Mitch, but Denzil and Leroy came in and asked if I had worked on a black Jeep Grand Cherokee with damage to the front right fender. I told them I hadn't seen anything like it. Since I wanted to get as much out of them as possible, I started asking them some questions."

"Well, what kinds of questions, Rufus? I hope like hell your questions didn't raise any suspicions. And where the hell was my Jeep when they came by?"

Rufus was clearly enjoying this conversation with Mitch. Seeing the arrogant Mitch McMasters rattled was a rare sight, and good ole Rufus Jones was the only person getting to see the show. "Calm down, Mitch, I played it cool. And your damn Jeep was in the back shed, covered up with a blue tarp."

"Are you sure, Rufus?"

"Hell, yes, Mitch. They dropped by asked some questions and left. They didn't go over to the shed. The weeds are too damn high for one thing, and it was hot that day. Those boys are too damn lazy to take a hot walk, unless they were ordered to."

"So what else did they tell you?"

"Well, they let it slip that it involved a death investigation. A hit and run deal. Does any of this ring a bell, Mitch?"

"You know, Rufus, you can go to hell for all I care. I wasn't involved in a hit and run. Well, not that type of hit and run."

"Ok, Mitch, but how many hit and runs have there been lately that both involved a 2008 Jeep Grand Cherokee?" There was a long pause before Mitch said anything. Rufus continued with his story. "Yeah, they are not only looking for a black Jeep Grand Cherokee, they have some expert who has it down to a 2008 black Jeep Grand Cherokee. Isn't that something, Mitch?"

Mitch sat in silence with a strange blank stare. Rufus could see Mitch's fingers were shaking as he tried to grip the steering wheel of his car. Rufus let the silence sink in before he sealed his financial deal with Mitch. As they pulled into Rufus' fine business establishment, Rufus presented his deal to Mitch, "Listen, you are in a real mess. I don't know all the details; but when the cops are looking for ya, it's not good. Here's the deal, $10,000 in cash tomorrow and $5,000 every month until you are out of trouble. I won't say a damn thing. But if anything ever happens to me, there will be a map heading right to you. If you think I'm kidding around, then head that way at your peril. This is some serious shit, and I'm not joking around, Mitch."

Mitch knew that he was in no position to bargain or to try to gain some competitive advantage. For one of the few times in his adult life, Mitch McMasters was beat and he damn well knew it. He started to quiz Rufus about what he meant about the map heading to him, but he decided that it would be best to let that one slide. He agreed to the terms of the surrender of his finances along with his self esteem and cursed himself as he glanced at Rufus from the rearview mirror of his luxury car as he left Rufus Jones' fine establishment.

CLARE McMASTERS awoke nearly two hours after Mitch had left their palatial estate in Bouvier. Despite having spent the night on the sofa in their den, she was well rested and in good spirits. Clare had been so tired the prior evening, both physically and emotionally, that she had no idea when

Mitch came home last night or when he had left that morning. The rest had done some good. Clare didn't feel like she was walking in a fog, as she had felt since she had learned of Haley's death. Maybe venting the prior afternoon had helped as well. She had her usual morning dose of coffee, showered, and was out the door for work by 7:45 a.m. Even though she spent very little time getting ready that morning, Clare still looked as beautiful as ever. She had a natural beauty and grace that enabled her to look her best in almost any situation.

As she drove to work, Clare kept replaying her confrontational conversations the prior day with Blanche Murtrey and Sammy Burger. It was so out of character for Clare to act out in such a manner that she was greatly bothered by her conduct toward both ladies. As she was about to reach the offices of the Bouvier Gazette, Clare dialed the number for the Sheriff's office. She immediately reached Sammy Burger, who rightfully So was not happy to hear Clare's voice. But Sammy was pleasantly caught off guard by what Clare had to say. Sammy was genuinely grateful for Clare's apology. Once they had concluded their short conversation, Clare asked to speak to Buford Blakeley. Clare wanted to let Buford know that she was sincerely sorry for her conduct toward Sammy.

As soon as Buford got on the phone with Clare, it was evident to her that something was wrong with Buford. Despite Buford's gruff introduction, Clare decided to trudge on with her prepared apology. Once she was done, the response from Buford totally threw Clare for a loop.

"Well, Miss Clare, I appreciate the kind words and all; but when you said you were calling to apologize, I figured it was for the press release." A perplexed Clare had no idea what Buford was talking about.

"Buford, I hate to be dumb at this moment, but I have no idea what you are talking about."

"The damn press release, Clare you left out the most important part."

"Buford, I ran it exactly the way you wrote it. A lot of newspapers would edit down a lengthy press release, but I ran it verbatim. Buford, I think you are mistaken about the coverage of your press release."

"Like hell I am. You edited out the description of the damn car. Now I look like a dumb ass because I have people asking me this morning, 'Do you have any information on the mystery car? How can we help if you don't have any damn specifics for the mystery car?' That's the kind of shit I have had to endure so far this morning thanks to your selective editing."

"So Buford, you are telling me that our article about the investigation left out the description of the car?"

"You're damn right it did."

"I have not been to the office yet, so I have not seen the final edition of last night's paper. If it's not in there, I will owe you an apology. But I know however, I ran it exactly as you wrote it."

"I will be hearing from you shortly. Have a good day, Clare."

"Thanks a lot, Buford."

Clare hurriedly parked her car and made a dash into the *Gazette* building. As soon as she entered the building, the staff could tell something was up when Clare barked out, "I need today's edition, now!" Unlike most days, she didn't say hello or good morning, or any other salutation. A staffer handed her the latest edition of the *Bouvier Gazette* and Clare immediately started reading the front page article about the investigation into Haley's wreck. Once she got to the part with the press release, Clare became very emotional. She threw down the paper and yelled, "Who changed the article about Haley? I need to know ASAP, who changed the article I wrote about the wreck investigation?"

There was total silence in the newsroom of the *Gazette*. Most of the staff had worked with Clare for over ten years, and none had ever seen her react in such an emotional way. They were shocked to see her yelling and crying about a mistake in an article.

"I cannot believe this. How could this happen? The sheriff is really upset because he thinks I doctored his press release. If anyone here changed the article, please let me know now. I really need to know." Once again silence filled the newsroom. Clare glanced around the newsroom with tears rolling down her cheeks and softly said, "I'm sorry, I'm sorry," as she made her way to her office. Once she got to her office she shut the door and buried her head in her hands and cried for what seemed to be an eternity.

After regaining her composure, Clare called the sheriff and made amends for the mistake. She honestly and sincerely told Buford that she had keyed in the press release exactly as it had been provided. She did not know how or who created the change. Clare offered to run it again in the next issue of the *Gazette*, without any editing errors. Buford accepted Clare's offer and her apology. But he was keenly suspicious of how the description of the car went missing from the paper. Buford's gut feeling was that Clare was telling the truth. But he suspicioned that Mitch was some way able to make the change in the news release without Clare knowing.

AFTER DEALING with Rufus Jones, a distraught Mitch McMasters made his way to the lake cabin. He had decided that a day of boating and drinking were in order. In light of his mood, combined with the fact that he had nothing scheduled, boating and drinking on a beautiful September day seemed to be a great way to spend the day. After dealing with a couple of maintenance matters at the boat dock, Mitch finished packing his needed items for his day on the lake. A fully iced down cooler of Budweiser was the most important item for Mitch to pack for his day. Mitch threw in a couple of sandwiches, some chips, and grabbed a bottle of sunscreen due to the bright sunshine. He was ready for the day and his mood was starting to lift. Just as he was leaving the cabin, Mitch glanced down at his cell phone. It showed two missed calls. One was from Clare, and the other was from his long-time attorney, Raleigh J. Calhoun. Mitch thought, "Oh, great," as he saw the calls. He assumed the worst when he saw Clare's call, but a call from Raleigh was unexpected.

An unexpected call from Raleigh J. Calhoun was never good news. At least that was the case, as long as Mitch had known Raleigh. Mr. Calhoun had been providing legal services for the McMasters family and the *Bouvier Gazette* for over thirty years. In fact, Raleigh had been a drinking buddy of Mitch's father. However, he had never taken a liking to Mitch. He tolerated Mitch, but that was as far as their relationship went. Through the years Mitch had become fully aware of Raleigh's attitude toward him. Mitch had considered ditching Raleigh for a more friendly legal counsel, but his good sense persuaded him to do otherwise. Raleigh knew all of the family secrets, and he was quite good at his vocation. Deep down Mitch didn't want to place his legal fate in someone else's hands. So he and Raleigh continued their uncomfortable dance, which meant they tolerated each other for strictly business reasons.

Mitch couldn't stomach a confrontation with Clare, especially after what he had just gone through with Rufus. But he knew better than to blow off Raleigh J. Calhoun. Reluctantly called Raleig, whose secretary said that Mr. Calhoun was expecting his call and would be with him shortly. Mitch thought, "Great, he's expecting my call. This cannot be good."

Within a few seconds, Mitch heard a deep slow voice, which had a distinct flat Ozarks accent. It was the voice of Raleigh J. Calhoun.

"Mitch, thanks for calling. We need to meet and the sooner the better."

Mitch was caught off guard by Raleigh's invitation and he hesitantly replied, "Ok, Raleigh, but what the hell is going on?"

"I was contacted this morning by Forrest Gamble, an attorney in Castle Rock. Forrest represents a client, who would like to enter into a business agreement, so to speak, with you."

"You know, Raleigh, I don't know what the hell you are talking about. So try a little simple English with me. Maybe I will understand that."

"Mitch, are you conversing on a cell phone. As your legal counsel, I strongly suggest that you get your ass in my office to discuss this matter. I will not discuss this over the phone. How about you drop by in the next thirty minutes?"

A pissed off Mitch McMasters could only muster a, "No problem," reply back to Raleigh. His day of boating and drinking were now on the ropes. Hopefully, Raleigh wouldn't totally destroy the entire day.

MITCH arrived at the esteemed law office of Raleigh J. Calhoun within twenty minutes of their phone conversation.

He sat in one of the leather chairs, which helped decorate the waiting area of the Calhoun Law Firm. Raleigh had a strong liking to the Southern colonial designs, and it clearly showed in his law office. He had by far the most impressive law office of any attorney in Bouvier. Partly because he was the most successful of his legal brethren in the town, but also because of his sense of Southern style and culture. Being a child of the South, Mississippi to be exact, Raleigh never let go of his love of things southern, even though he had lived in the Ozarks of Southwest Missouri for over thirty years. He had come to Bouvier because his wife was from the area. Over time he grew to love the unique way of life in the Ozarks; but deep down, Raleigh longed to be in his beloved Mississippi.

After waiting for five minutes, which seemed like five hours, Mitch was shown back to Raleigh's rather impressive private office. Mitch hated Raleigh's office for many reasons. First, was the fact that he did not like Raleigh. Secondly, he was jealous of the exquisite design of the office, from the carpet all the way down to the stylish holder for Raleigh's pens and pencil. And finally, it was the most intimidating office in Bouvier, which was something that Raleigh knew and cherished, even though he tried to nonchalantly brush it off when it would come up in discussions from time to time.

Raleigh met Mitch in his usual southern grace and charm. Raleigh was elegantly dressed in a blue and white seersucker suit, white starched shirt, black dress loafers, and his beloved red and blue Ole Miss tie. A graduate of the University of Mississippi law school, the red and blue tie, which adorned the Ole Miss symbol, was standard attire for Raleigh on each Friday during football season. Mitch hated Raleigh's Ole Miss tie, especially since Ole Miss had beaten the University of Missouri four out of the last five times they had played football, which was very seldom. Mizzou had won the last outing, but Mitch still hated the tie. Deep down he knew it had more to do with his feelings for Raleigh than the outcome of a college football game. Raleigh was in his late fifties, slightly overweight, and had a beautiful full head of gray hair, which gave him quite the dashing look. He still caught the eye of women around town, but he was totally devoted and faithful to his beautiful and elegant wife of thirty-three years, Charlyn Belle Calhoun.

The door to Raleigh's office was immediately closed, and Raleigh sat down at his impressive mahogany desk. He placed his reading glasses on the edge of his nose where he gave the appearance of peering down at his client. After clearing his throat, with his deep and slow delivery, Raleigh began to explain why he had called Mitch to his office on such short notice. As Mitch sat there waiting for Raleigh to begin his presentation, he thought once again about why he hated coming to see Raleigh. Raleigh was always in control, and this was one of the few places in Bouvier where Mitch didn't have a competitive advantage.

"Mitch, you look like death warmed over on this beautiful morning."

"Yeah, thanks, Raleigh, you have no idea what's going on in my life right now. So save me the critique of my personal appearance. I hope that wasn't why you demanded my appearance this morning."

"No, unfortunately it is not why I called. Mitch, this morning I received a rather startling communication from Forrest Gamble, who as you well know, is an attorney in Castle Rock. Forrest mainly does real estate work. However, he does represent several businesses in the lake area. Apparently, one of his clients is Pate Johnston, with whom I am sure you are acquainted. Pate owns the Eagle Crest Resort on the lake. Well, Pate apparently got with Forrest and had Forrest draft an offer of a confidentiality agreement with you."

A rather perplexed Mitch McMasters blurted out, "What the hell are you talking about, Raleigh? Save me the bull shit and get to the damn point." Mitch's outburst didn't appear to rattle Raleigh at all as he slowly continued his presentation.

"The offer of confidentiality covers actions that Pate's daughter, Kate, saw take place between you and the late Haley Fulz. Specifically, Kate claims she witnessed you and the late Ms. Fulz, who was the age of seventeen at the time of the acts described, engaged in sexual activities on the screened-in porch of your lake house on more than one occasion in the month of August of this year." Raleigh stopped at this point to let his words sink in and to gage the reaction of his client.

Mitch sat speechless and red faced. He just shook his head, then tilted it back, and yelled out, "That gutless bastard! You know I would at least respect Ole Pate a little bit if he had the guts to shake me down in person, you know, face to face."

"So I assume from your response that their accusation is true."

"O screw you Raleigh. I don't want to talk about what I did or didn't do right now. I want to talk abou,t their offer and what kind of protection it can give me. So how much are they trying to shake me down for?"

"Fifty thousand now and twenty thousand a year for the next four years."

"This is blackmail. I knew Pate was having financial problems with the resort, but I had no idea he was so desperate that he would resort to blackmail to save his ass. It looks like my attorney could do something about a blackmail attempt."

Raleigh smiled at Mitch's attempt to slam him. It was more of a "you annoy me, you childish brat" smile.

"Well, Mitch we can certainly alert the authorities and let Ernie sort everything out to determine if a blackmail charge is warranted. It's what I would recommend. I have read the offer three times, and Forrest did an excellent job of drafting the offer in such a manner that avoids blackmail or obstruction of justice."

"Maybe I should hire Forrest to represent me from now on. It looks like he knows how to keep a person out of trouble."

"Be my guest, Mitch. The only problem is that you wouldn't be in that seat if you hadn't been screwing a seventeen year old girl, who if I recall correctly, was your son's steady girlfriend. I didn't create your problem Mitch,; you did. So I suggest you take your arrogant attitude down to Forrest's office and let him defend your sorry ass. Do you still want me to get Ernie on the phone to pursue the blackmail claim?" In an effort to further piss off Mitch, Raleigh reached for his phone, as if he were about to place a call to Ernie Lambert's office.

"Ok, ok, Raleigh, I get the point. Are you done with your lecture? It's amazing that I pay you dearly so that you can treat me like crap."

"Mitch, I have better things to do than to deal with your infantile attitude. I will notify Forrest that you have decided to retain other counsel. Good day, Mitch."

"Ok, Raleigh, I get it. What do we do from here? As you can see, I cannot let this get out. But is a confidentiality agreement really worth a damn?"

"As far as enforcement, this one is rather one sided. If you agree to their offer, it is a legally enforceable contract. If you don't pay, they can sue you and obtain a judgment as long as they have performed their contractual vow of confidentiality.

In other words, they keep their damn mouth shut. On your side of the coin, it gets tricky. If you enter into the agreement with them and they end up telling people about what they saw, you can sue. However, they are banking on the fear factor of you not wanting this matter to be paraded around in a courtroom. I would recommend that a provision be added that enforcement of any breaches be handled only by arbitration. It would still be a semi-public matter, but it wouldn't be in a court of law. The other problem is the scope of their required confidentiality. It does not cover direct questioning during law enforcement or judicial actions. In other words, if Kate is questioned by the law or has to go to court and is asked about the matter, she will tell the truth."

"So what the hell does it do for me, if they will tell the truth, if questioned?"

"It would require them not to go into town and tell anyone they want to tell about you screwing a seventeen year old girl. Also, it would keep them from initiating contact with law enforcement officials. That's where Forrest did an excellent job of keeping this from becoming an obstruction of justice document. They will not initiate contact with law enforcement officials. But if they are contacted by a law enforcement officer, they would honestly answer direct questions. He did use the word direct, when talking about questions from law enforcement officers. So it has some merit. But one of the numerous questions I have is, did Kate sneak up on you and Haley by herself, or did she have someone with her? Also, I find it hard to believe she wouldn't tell anyone before they reached this agreement. It's against human nature, especially the nature of a seventeen year old girl, not to tell others if they had just seen something like this."

"In other words, it's not worth much."

"Probably not. It's kind of like trying to stop the leak in a dam. Just when you think you've got everything fixed, another leak appears out of nowhere. The best it would do is provide you some short term peace and quiet. I would suspect that Kate was not alone and has already told a few other people. But there is one good thing Mitch."

"What the hell is that Raleigh?"

"At least she was seventeen. Otherwise, you could be facing a second degree statutory rape charge."

"Screw you, Raleigh."

"Is there anything else you would like to discuss regarding the late Ms. Fulz?"

Mitch paused, took a long look out the window of Raleigh's office, and then he dejectedly shook his head and quietly said, "No, not at this time."

"Mitch, are you sure? Because you take what we have just discussed, combined with the article in your paper today makes me think you are in some deep trouble. I understand the sheriff is pissed off at your wife for editing out the description of the mystery vehicle."

As expected, the remark hit Mitch hard. Red faced and fearful, Mitch shot back, "Where the hell did you hear that?"

"Mitch, I have my sources. The sheriff is pissed. So you take an eye witness to you and Haley screwing, the rumor that she was pregnant, combined with the Sheriff looking for a Jeep Grand Cherokee, which just so happens to be the same kind of vehicle owned by you; and add all these details together and this looks really bad for you, Mitch."

Mitch was visibly shaken by what he had just heard from his own attorney. "Dammit! Ok, you remove the eyewitness and things improve. Confirm with that damn Forrest that Kate was the only one involved in the snooping."

"Ok, then what?"

"I don't know. Or, I could go have a long talk with that chicken shit Pate Johnston."

"Mitch, I wouldn't recommend that. The final provision of the offer states basically that if anything suspicious were to happen to the Johnston family or if any means of intimidation are attempted against the Johnston family, all of the information at their disposal will be delivered by Forrest Gamble to the proper authorities. In other words, they mean business. Mess with us and you will pay and pay dearly."

"Great, this is just great. I need to think. I will talk to you later."

With that Mitch emotionally staggered out of the office of Raleigh J. Calhoun. Raleigh couldn't help but snicker at the plight of his spoiled brat client, who was for once not getting his way.

ONCE he had finally left the office of Raleigh J. Calhoun, Mitch glanced down at his cell phone and saw three missed calls and messages from Clare. He knew this was not good. After dealing with Rufus Jones, Raleigh J. Calhoun, and a shake down attempt by Pate Johnston, Mitch couldn't take a fight with Clare. He turned his phone off for two hours and headed for the lake. Mitch McMasters needed time to think about his future and how to handle the various problems headed his way. He would deal with Clare later, when his head was clearer and his self esteem was stronger. Plus, he had to round up the cash to pay Rufus. It was not one of his better days.

CHAPTER 15

BUFORD BLAKLEY was enjoying the lunch special at Ruby's when his cell phone rang. It was the Sheriff's office and Buford wasn't happy. His secretary was under strict instructions not to bother him during lunch at Ruby's unless there was an emergency. The ongoing problem between Buford and his secretary was her definition of an emergency. Buford took a much more narrow approach to the definition of an emergency, especially on days that Ruby's was serving barbecued brisket, fried chicken, or barbecued ribs.

Buford was just about to take a bite of his chicken fried chicken, which was smothered with white gravy, when he heard his secretary, Sammy Burger's voice. Initially, he was annoyed; but after hearing what she had to say, his mood changed. Buford quickly finished his chicken fried chicken, mashed potatoes, green beans, and raspberry cobbler and made his way out of Ruby's as fast as possible without giving the appearance that he was in a hurry. A hurried Sheriff always raises questions from the good ole boys about what's going on. Buford didn't want to answer any questions today. He was still pissed off about how the *Bouvier Gazette* messed up his press release, and he was afraid he might say something at the Ruby's board table that he would regret. So he ate and promptly left.

Sammy Burger had received a phone call from a young man who had seen the article in the *Bouvier Gazette* about the investigation into Haley Fulz's death. The man said he had information that would help with the investigation. He said that he was pleasantly surprised there was an investigation. The person who called didn't want to give his name, but he did give his cell phone number, but only on the condition that only the sheriff call him back. He did not want to talk to anyone but the sheriff. His quote to Sammy was, "I don't trust anyone but the sheriff."

Buford Blakeley immediately called the cell phone number provided to him. Within three rings he heard the voice mail of a man who identified himself as Brandon. Brandon sounded like he was in his late teens. Buford left a short message and impatiently waited for a return call. Forty-five minutes later, Buford's cell phone rang again. This time it was the cell number for Brandon. Brandon asked the sheriff if he was alone, and Buford confirmed that was the case. He then asked the sheriff if they could meet, but he would meet only with the sheriff and no one else. Buford agreed to the request. Brandon gave specific instructions for the meeting spot. It happened to be a very remote section of the vast Roaring River State Park, not far from the spot of Haley's death. Brandon asked Buford to meet him there in thirty minutes. He concluded the call by stating, "If you try to bring anyone else with you, I will be gone before you can get to the meeting spot."

AS INSTRUCTED, Buford drove straight to the meeting spot requested by Brandon at the precise time of the appointment. After waiting seven minutes, a young man appeared from nowhere. Brandon, or whatever his actual name was, stood about five feet ten inches tall, weighted around 175, had flowing black hair. Other than a one day's growth of a beard, he appeared to be a very handsome, clean cut kid. Buford estimated Brandon to be around twenty years of age. By his attire Buford quickly concluded that Brandon worked at the state park. This was why he had been able to appear without a sound.

Buford reached out and shook Brandon's hand. "Son, I appreciate the call. What can I do for you? I guess I should say, what can you do for me?"

"Sheriff, I was quite surprised and pleased to see in the *Gazette* that you are investigating Haley's death?"

"Why's that?"

"Well, car wrecks happen all the time. I just expected this one would be chalked up as another person driving too fast on these dangerous curves. Whatever the reason, I'm glad you are looking into Haley's death. I'm glad, but at the same time I'm also nervous about the investigation."

"Brandon, for many reasons Haley's wreck didn't make sense to me. So we decided to take a further look to make sure it wasn't just the usual car driving out of control situation. Why are you nervous about our investigation?"

"I knew Haley well, probably too well. I know who was involved with her. I'm not comfortable with them knowing that I am talking to you and what I am talking about. Plus, from the time I started working here at the park a couple of years ago, I have seen a lot of things that I never dreamed took place in this county. In other words, I do not feel safe telling you anything unless everything I tell you stays just with you and Ernie Lambert."

"Son, I guess I don't understand what you are talking about. Why don't you feel safe talking to me?"

"First things first, you have a guy on your staff who is on the take with the local meth dealers, among others."

"Really, who do you think is on the take?"

"Sheriff, I lead you in the right direction. But you should have a hunch who it is. If you don't, then I am not going to waste my time telling you anything. Because if you don't have a clue who it is, then that confirms my fear that you can't keep me safe."

"Dammit son, I am not about to start divulging what I know and what I don't know about my staff to a total stranger that I just met less than fifteen minutes ago. I am not that stupid. Give me something to go on, or I'm heading back up the big hill and going home."

"You have a special agent who works for you and the state police on drug cases. He nailed a couple of meth labs last week. They wouldn't play his game. But he also let a couple off the hook recently because they paid to play. He has a go between, however, who makes the deals. This way he is clean with the meth dealers. His go between is as dirty as they come."

The information Brandon had just given Buford had confirmed the suspicions Buford had held for some time about special agent, Alex Vander. Alex, known as A.V., was a long-time special agent for the county and the state police. He had been clean most of his career. but the allure of making some big money off the meth dealers was too good to be true. An old meth dealer hatched the plan to shakedown the meth cartel, and he pitched it to Alex. Alex saw his 401k balances shrinking each month. He was approaching retirement age, and the plan began to look even better. Over the past two years, Alex Vander and his cohort had raked in over three hundred thousand dollars in bribes from the county's meth dealers. All of it was tax free, and they had evenly split their windfall. Alex figured that two more years and he would be able to retire, and no one would have to know about his crimes. For over a year Buford had developed a strong suspicion that A.V. was up to something. However,he had never been able to figure out who his partner was in their scheme. If this kid was right, this could be his opportunity to blow A.V. and the Barry County meth cartel totally out of the water. Buford leaned forward and asked Brandon, "I have a lot of guys cover the park area. Does A.V. come through the park very often?"

Brandon smiled because he had just been given the code he was looking for and replied, "He does quite often. A.V. seems to be prospering these days."

"Brandon, you have thrown a lot at me in a very short time period. First, you have information regarding Haley's death, and you know about a scheme to allow the free flow of meth in the county. Where do you want to start, Brandon? I assume you are going to tell us there is some sort of tie between the death and the meth scheme? Also is it safe to assume that Brandon isn't your real name?"

"No, Brandon isn't my real name. You are clearly tracking in the right direction and will get it and the rest of my story once I can confirm I haven't been compromised by meeting with you today."

"What the hell are you talking about being compromised, Brandon, or whatever the hell your name is?"

"I called your secretary and told her I wanted to talk to you and you only about the Haley Fulz investigation. The only other information I gave her was the name Brandon and a cell number. If that information has been passed around your department, I can guarantee you I will receive a call on this cell phone within twenty four hours."

"So I take it this isn't your cell phone.

"No, it's Brandon's, not mine."

"Where's Brandon?"

"He comes and goes. He's gone for the moment. Ok, here's the deal. If no one approaches me in the next twenty-four hours, I will contact you and let you know the whole story. It will be worth the wait. But the next meeting I would prefer to include Ernie Lambert."

"No problem, Brandon. So you will contact me? What if Ernie doesn't want to play it that way?"

"If you push me right now, I can disappear and you will never find me. So I suggest you agree to be patient for the next day. I promise you it will be worth the wait."

"It damn well better be." At this point the sheriff heard his police radio requesting his assistance. He walked to the police cruiser and spoke with an officer for less than a minute. When he finished, Buford realized that he was all alone in the deep woods of Roaring River State Park. In less than a minute the young man calling himself Brandon vanished almost into thin air. Buford hurried into his car and flew up the steep park hill and headed straight for Ernie Lambert's office. As he was driving, he desperately hoped Brandon would call again and that Ernie would believe his story. Buford hadn't been this excited since his single dating days. Hopefully, the return call would be more reliable than they were in Buford's dating days. Within ten minutes Buford was regaling Ernie Lambert with his tale. After hearing it, Ernie knew he wouldn't be able to sleep any that night. Brandon's story was almost too good to be true.

THE FRIDAY afternoon barbecue on the balcony of Raleigh J. Calhoun's law office, overlooking the clear flowing blue water of the beautiful Flat Creek, was a tradition for the members of the Bouvier legal community. Raleigh would hold the barbecues during football season and sometimes in the spring, except for the weekends when he was attending an Ole Miss home football game. Typically by 3 p.m. the smell of barbecue smoke swept through the air. Soon thereafter, the beer would begin to flow. Things never got out of hand. But it was a great way to finish a stressful week. Needless to say, the court dockets at the Barry County Courthouse cleared out most Friday afternoons during this time of the year, as Raleigh's beer and barbecue were highly sought after affairs. So much so, that visiting judges would purposely ask for a fall docket so they could be in Bouvier during Raleigh's barbecue season. The affairs were dominated by the usual stuff: gossip, football, and a little legal shop talk.

The Bouvier legal community was dictated by Mizzou alums, with a few Arkansas fans thrown in. Raleigh stood proudly as the lone Ole Miss Rebel of the bunch. As far as Raleigh was concerned, the greatest quarterback in the history of the game was the former Rebel, Archie Manning, who was followed closely by his son, Eli Manning. When Peyton Manning chose the University of Tennessee over Ole Miss, it nearly killed Raleigh. But Eli's success tenure at Ole Miss greatly soothed Raleigh's wounds.

Raleigh loved football season, barbecue, beer, and sharing all three with his buddies in the Bouvier legal community. He loved to barbecue ribs, chicken, pork steaks, and burgers. You could always count on barbecued pork steaks on the weekend of the Ole Miss-Arkansas game. As an ongoing prank, Raleigh would always overcook and badly burn a couple of pork steaks and serve them to his Arkansas Razorback buddies. This Friday the entrée could be barbecue ribs.

Ernie Lambert was a trusted friend to Raleigh. In fact, Raleigh had helped mentor Ernie when he came to Bouvier. However, Ernie seldom attended Raleigh's barbecues, primarily because he detested a couple of lawyers and one judge who regularly attended the function. Nevertheless, Ernie wasn't going to miss this Friday's affair. He knew Raleigh was serving his legendary ribs, and he never missed Raleigh's rib fest. Secondly, if Brandon's story had hit anyone's radar screen, it would slip out after a couple of beers at Raleigh's. And he wanted to be there to gauge the reaction to the press release about Haley's death. Gossipy attorneys sometimes ended up blurting out useful information.

As was the custom, all the usual parties arrived by 3 p.m., and the charcoal grill was ablaze. Beers were being opened and the ribs could be seen in the kitchen area being seasoned prior to being placed on the fire. The only thing out of the ordinary was Raleigh, who never mixed legal business with his legendary barbecues, but today was the exception. When Ernie arrived, a couple of his attorney friends pulled him to the side and whispered the news that Raleigh was tied up in some negotiation. He would apparently be freed up within thirty minutes. Little did Ernie know how much Raleigh's negotiations might impact his investigation into Haley Fulz death.

Between Mitch's brain storming session at the lake and a couple of well placed phone calls by Raleigh, a plan had been hatched to alleviate Mitch's fears regarding Kate Johnston's bird's eye knowledge of his affair with Haley. After upping his price for confidentiality, Pate Johnston would be closing down their resort the following day, which was three weeks earlier than usual, and temporarily move his family in with his well-to-do sister in Destin, Florida. As a result, on Monday morning Kate Johnston would be enrolling for classes at the nearby Santa Rosa High School and finish her senior year of high school on the white sandy beaches of Florida. Only time would tell how long it would take Kate the party girl to find trouble in the thriving tourist destinations of Destin, Ft. Walton, and Panama City Beach. Of course, this was of little concern to Mitch McMasters. He would have the star witness to his demise 900 miles away from Bouvier. She could go join a cult for all he cared. She would be gone and hopefully soon to be forgotten. The Johnstons were under strict guidelines under their agreement not to divulge where they were moving. Mitch had back loaded his agreement, so there was strong incentive for the Johnston family to simply enjoy life in Florida and to keep their mouths shut.

Raleigh had been able to unearth the existence of Kate's accessory in her spy operation of Mitch and Haley. He quickly discovered that neither Morgan Langley nor her parents wanted anything to do with Mitch McMasters' situation. Raleigh's offer of $50,000 reinforced their desire to lay low about the affair. Morgan's parents had good jobs, but an extra $50,000 right before Morgan started to college was nothing to sneeze at. Plus, Morgan's parents delighted in getting the money out of someone they totally detested. If they had known the affair had led to Haley's death, they wouldn't have taken the money. At that point they had no idea of the connection.

By 3:30 p.m. Raleigh had concluded the agreements and was ready for a beer. Unfortunately, having dealt with Mitch McMasters all day had caused him to lose his appetite. Raleigh had completed a skillful legal maneuver in his representation of Mitch McMasters, but he was not proud of his actions that day. Deep down inside, Raleigh believed that Mitch deserved everything the good Lord had in store for him for his sophomoric actions with a seventeen year old girl. After his first Budweiser, Raleigh's nerves had calmed; but Ernie Lambert could tell that something was on his dear friend's mind. In time, he would learn what was keeping Raleigh preoccupied on that beautiful day in September. By 5:00 p.m. Ernie had finished his incredible ribs and two Budweisers. During his time at Raleigh's, not a word had been spoken about the Haley Fulz investigation. Ernie went home and planned his next legal moves for the investigation over the weekend.

CHAPTER 16

CLARE McMASTERS had attempted and failed to contact Mitch McMasters all day Friday. Their marriage had deteriorated to the point where she was only mildly concerned that he could not be contacted for over twelve hours. She wanted to reach him more out of anger than concern. She suspected that Mitch had changed the article about the investigation into Haley's death. Clare was embarrassed, angry, and ready for a direct confrontation with her inattentive husband.

Around 7:00 p.m. on Friday evening, Clare found Mitch in a drunken stupor at their lake cabin. By the looks of things, he had downed more beers than she cared to count. He was breathing and appeared to be ok physically. However, due to the level of beer consumed, Mitch was out for the evening. Clare was disappointed, as she was ready to put some things on the table, verbally so to speak, that had been bothering her for years. Now, due to his drunken, selfish behavior, Mitch couldn't face what Clare had prepared for him that evening.

Clare began to pace back and forth in the cabin. She wanted no part of the place as it was clearly Mitch's domain, but she was inquisitive as to what he had been doing that day and every day. Clare went to the room, which served as Mitch's lake office, and found a legal pad on his desk. There were few legible markings on the pad, except for the office number for Raleigh J. Calhoun, the phone number for the trust officer for the McMasters Trust financial holdings, and the scribbling,

"Wire money to Destin National Bank." Clare read the findings over and over to make sure she saw them correctly. After about five minutes, she left the cabin and her drunken husband and made a mad dash to Bouvier.

On her way back to town, Clare reached Raleigh J. Calhoun at his home. Ole Miss was playing on the road that weekend, so Raleigh was home enjoying the beautiful September night with his lovely wife Charlyn Belle Calhoun. Clare hated to interrupt Raleigh's evening, but she needed someone to talk to at the moment, both from a personal and legal standpoint. Raleigh and Charlyn Belle had become close trusted friends to Clare. Their feelings for Clare were vastly different than what they held for Mitch. After assuring Clare that she was not interrupting anything important, Clare asked Raleigh if she could come over to their home for a short talk. Raleigh immediately agreed, for he could sense Clare was upset. Now he was wishing he had not been so skillful earlier in the day in his representation of Mitch.

Clare arrived at the Calhoun's beautiful southern colonial home, which was located at the south end of Bouvier on five manicured acres. With the carefully placed floodlights illuminating the front, the two story brick home with large white columns had a regal look that evening. The locals often joked that Raleigh may have left Mississippi, but he brought part of it back with him when he and Charlyn Belle built their home.

Charlyn Belle was a local girl who met Raleigh through a friend who had gone to the University of Mississippi. She was six years younger than Raleigh. Her father had been a businessman in Bouvier, and she enticed Raleigh to set up his legal practice in Bouvier upon his graduation from Ole Miss Law School. It was a move that Raleigh had never regretted. He loved Mississippi, but he loved Charlyn Belle more. Over time Raleigh began to feel right at home in the beautiful Ozarks of Southwest Missouri. The southern styled home helped Raleigh ease his natural longing for Mississippi. They lived alone in their home as they never had children. The reason for which had never been openly discussed by either Raleigh or Charlyn Belle.

WHEN CHARLYN greeted Clare McMasters at the door of their elegant home, it was quite clear that Clare was deeply distraught. The two, long-time friends warmly hugged; and Charlyn offered Clare something to drink. Charlyn was known in her circle of friends for a killer recipe for Margaritas and Clare could not resist one on this evening. Dressed in a casual v-neck black blouse and jeans, Charlyn was as elegant and gracefully sexy as ever. Her beautiful black hair was pulled back and she appeared to be relaxed for a quiet evening. Even though she was in her early fifties, she could easily pass for being in her late twenties or early thirties. She loved to be carded by checkers at the local supermarket when purchasing a bottle of tequila or some beer. Usually the young male clerks were the ones who occasionally asked Charlyn Belle for her driver's license when she was buying alcohol beverages. Her friends enviously said the clerks were just flirting with her when they asked for her ID. Regardless, she loved it.

While Charlyn was getting the Margaritas, Raleigh made his way into their front sitting room. Dressed in a pair of khaki shorts, a blue sports shirt, and sandels, Raleigh could immediately tell that Clare was an emotional wreck. She gave Raleigh a tight hug that tacitly spoke volumes to her need to have a strong person give her some solid advice. After some brief small talk, Clare asked if they could speak in his private home office as she needed to some advice, which could be considered to be confidential and of legal nature. Raleigh knew this was coming, and he gladly accommodated Clare's request. Charlyn brought Clare her drink and Raleigh another Budweiser and excused herself so they could talk business.

Clare and Raleigh sat down in the leather chairs, which occupied Raleigh's home office. His home office area was part law office and part library, which housed an enormous collection of great works of fiction, a favorite of Raleigh's. Charlyn had tastefully decorated it in a manner that was both warm and intimidating. After taking a few sips of her drink, Clare jumped in to explain why she had barged in Raleigh's house on a Friday evening.

"Raleigh, I cannot tell you how much I appreciate being able to talk to you tonight. I'm in a bad shape emotionally, and I desperately need some advice, both personal and legal." Clare went on to explain the events of the past two days, which were dominated by the press release from Buford Blakeley, her conversation with Chad, the missing portion of the press release in the paper, and the scribbled notes she had found at the lake cabin. She finished by stating, "Either I am very wrongly paranoid, or I correctly suspect my husband of being involved in Haley's accident or even more than just the accident."

Raleigh was in the very position he did not want to be in with regards to Clare. It was a position he had been in at various times of his career, due to the small town in which he practiced law and the demand for his skillful services. He had to walk a fine line not to break his client confidentiality with Mitch and potentially get disbarred and, at the same time, provide his other client, Clare, with sound advice.

"Clare I have to be perfectly honest with you. I represent Mitch as well as you. So I cannot discuss anything I have discussed with Mitch without his consent. With that said, I can give you some advice."

This statement initially stung Clare, but after a few seconds she regrouped and paused for her reply.

"Ok, I get ya Raleigh. Would you advise me to get checked at a psychiatric hospital for being delusionally paranoid?"

Raleigh shook his head and quietly said, "Not only no, but hell no."

Clare's eyes filled with tears and she said, "Thank you Raleigh. That's what I've been needing to hear. Do you know anything about the message Mitch had written down about wiring money to Destin National Bank?"

"I cannot discuss that. But let's do this; let's discuss your business at this moment. Is that ok?"

"I guess. I hope I understand where you are heading."

"Oh, you will, believe me, Clare, you will."

"So Raleigh, you cannot tell me anything about what Mitch is doing. Because you are helping him in whatever scheme he has to save his ass. Is that right?"

"Clare, let me be very clear. I represent Mitch. He has been a client for a long time. I also represent the newspaper, of which you now own half and are currently the president and secretary of the corporation. I know you don't like it, but I will not break attorney client privilege, regardless of my personal feelings for the client. If you will hear me out, I will give you some advice for your business, which should assist you greatly in the days ahead. But you have to help me here. We never had this conversation. Even the appearance of us meeting could be construed a lot of ways that would not be good for either of us. Do you understand?"

Clare began to cry. She knew her friend, Raleigh J. Calhoun, had just given her some bad news about her husband and her marriage, without even giving her an ounce of detail. At the same time, she knew Raleigh was prepared to help her in ways he probably shouldn't. She swallowed her pride and let Raleigh explain the next steps she should take with the newspaper's finances. He never once gave out privileged information, but Clare had a pretty good idea where Raleigh was headed.

Two hours later, a very distraught Clare McMasters left the home of Raleigh J. and Charlyn Belle Calhoun. She graciously thanked and apologized for taking up their Friday evening. As she drove to her home, she wondered if Mitch had ever awakened from his drunken stupor. She mischievously hoped he wouldn't wake up, but she couldn't be that lucky. At least she had a plan for Mitch, one that he wouldn't see coming and one that could severely impact his maneuvering.

CLARE McMASTERS started her Saturday morning bright and early with a 6:00 a.m. wake up by her trusty alarm clock. Despite feeling like her world that she had known her adult life was starting to crumble, she had no trouble getting up and around that morning. Being focused on her task at hand kept her sane, at the moment. She planned to go to the newspaper office and then to the Bouvier Community Bank, if the bank president, Carter Franklin, was available to meet with her. When she awoke, the first thing that ran through her mind was the condition of her drunken husband. She hoped he was battling the worst kind of hangover. She had her desperately needed cup of strong coffee and a bagel with cream cheese while she perused the regional daily newspapers. After a quick shower, Clare dressed and was at her office at the Bouvier

Gazette by 7:30 a.m. As she drove to town, she thought about calling Mitch to see how bad his hangover was, but decided her nerves could not take a confrontation at this moment. She had better things to do.

After working at her office for around an hour, Clare reached Carter Franklin on his cell phone. Clare apologized for the short notice as she asked if he would be free to meet with her before the bank closed at Noon. Carter said that he would rearrange a golf time and would meet her at his office at 10:30 a.m. Clare wasn't surprised by Carter's willingness to meet with her on such short notice on a Saturday morning. The *Bouvier Gazette* and the McMasters family had been customers of the Bouvier Community Bank for decades. Not only did Carter covet their banking relationship, he also loved the prestige that went with being the McMasters' banker.

As a second generation banker, Carter Franklin was known as a lazy and mediocre banker, who was more concerned with his social standing than representing the interests of the bank's stockholders. He was a notorious fence sitter, who had trouble making tough decisions, as he was always more concerned with his public image than what was the right business decision for the bank. Luckily for the stockholders of the bank, he had the good sense to hire a strong head of lending, who made the decisions that Carter tried to avoid. Carter also had the good fortune to marry the daughter of one of the leading stockholders in the Bouvier Community Bank. So regardless of how inept he was as a banker, Carter's job was pretty safe.

Always concerned with his image, Carter Franklin fretted about why Clare McMasters would want to meet with him on a Saturday morning. Before she arrived, he asked each of his officers on duty if they had upset the McMasters or if the

McMasters were upset with the bank for any reason. The word from each officer was they had no clue as to any problems with the family or the newspaper. Hearing this, Carter Franklin paced his office until Clare McMasters arrived.

Carter was dressed in a blue short sleeve golf shirt, which had a Bouvier Community Bank emblem, starched khakis, and brown loafers. He was appropriately dressed for the business occasion, sinse it was a Saturday, but Clare could immediately sense that Carter was uptight about their meeting. She knew he would be nervous, and she knew how he ran the bank, so that was why she wanted to meet with him privately. She understood that if she struck before Mitch knew what had happened to him and if she put the fear of God in Carter, she would be able to keep her banking transaction quiet and confidential. Otherwise, she knew Carter would be intimidated and manipulated by Mitch McMasters.

After a brief discussion about the beautiful weather, the Bouvier Cubs' football win, and her appreciation for Carter rearranging his golf match, Clare got to the business at hand. "Carter, what we discuss her today, must stay in this office. I hope you understand how serious I am about this. If you blab this outside the bank, I can guarantee you that I will know about it within the next twenty-four hours. If your wife knows what took place, then all of her golf clique will know as well and so will I. So Carter, if any of this is leaked by you or any of your staff, I will have you fired. You know I can make it happen. Are we clear?"

A terrified Carter Franklin was about to pee his khaki pants. For a candy-assed guy who hated making decisions, he hated confrontations even more. At this point Clare had clearly made her point quite clear, and there was no way Carter Franklin was going to take on Clare McMasters. He just nodded and waited for her next set of demands.

"Carter, as you can see from the newspaper's corporate documents, as president and secretary of *Bouvier Gazette*, Incorporated, I am authorized to handle all of the corporation's financial matters, including the line of credit." Carter was reeling, but he did have the guts to muster one question.

"Clare, I thought Mitch was the corporate president?"

"He was until two years ago. As you will remember, Mitch relinquished his position as corporate head of the *Gazette* when he became embroiled in a potential lawsuit over an accident on his boat. He settled the boat matter in some way or manner of his choosing, but he was never reinstated as president. I have copies of the most recent documentation filed with the Secretary of State's office." Clare politely handed over the documents to Carter. He quickly read them and then waited for Clare's next move.

"Carter, I need you to advance all of the available funds from the *Gazette's* line of credit and deposit them in the newspaper's investment account." When she said this, Carter's mouth literally dropped open.

"Clare, you want to draw the entire million dollar line of credit? May I ask for what reason?"

"Carter, you are correct. I want the full million dollars that are available in the line moved immediately to the investment account. The reason for the draw is for the newspaper to review investment and ownership options. Don't worry, the advance will be temporary." Clare and Raleigh had come up with the vague and meaningless term, "investment and ownership option." Clare was prepared to babble on with some other vague and meaningless dialog, which would thoroughly confuse and further intimidate poor ole Carter.

"Let me get this right. It's for investment and ownership options?"

"Exactly, Carter. I would love to go deeper into it, but the people I am dealing with have sworn all parties to total confidentiality. If any word of what we are doing gets out, I could be sued for a tremendous amount of money. As could you and the bank, since you are aware of the process from a cursory standpoint. I appreciate your consideration and discretion. I am confident you will handle this appropriately."

If Carter had possessed any gumption or guts, he wouldn't have let Clare off so easily, especially since he had the authority to approve or deny any advances on the credit line. A million dollar advance backed up by such a flimsy reason deserved further questions and scrutiny. But Clare knew there was no way Carter would hold up her request, even if it was a million dollar advance on a credit line, which was rarely used. The most that had ever been advanced on their line of credit in the past was $250,000, when the newspaper purchased new printing technology several years earlier.

The line of credit was set at $1,000,000 over twenty years earlier. The only reason the credit line was set up for a million was for ego purposes for both Mitch and his banker, at the time. Both conspired to set up the line, and they loved to crow around about the million dollar line of credit for the newspaper. Mitch would boast to his country club buddies that the bank practically begged him to take out the million dollar line; one that he would never need, since the paper was making so much money. His banker at the time, a rather arrogant and sleazy character named Danforth Graham, loved to brag to his bank board of directors that he had acquired for the bank a million dollar credit line, of which five other banks were in high pursuit. Both Mitch and Danforth deep down knew their respective stories were pure fiction, but they both loved knowing that together they had pulled off the financial transaction through gall and intimidation. Eventually, running with Mitch McMasters led to Danforth Graham's downfall. He began to embezzle funds from the bank to pay for the fast life of booze, gambling, and women he had developed from his friendship with Mitch. Danforth would go on to serve three years in a country club type federal prison for his embezzlement and was never seen again in Bouvier after his release.

After stumbling around for a few uncomfortable moments, Carter Franklin signed off on the loan advance. Clare McMasters left the bank a few minutes later as the proud owner of a million bucks in the newspapers investment account. Fearful that Mitch would intimidate an inexperienced teller into releasing funds to him, she had plans to move the money out of the Bouvier Community Bank. By the following Monday morning, the million dollars would be scattered to five banks in a three state area. After moving the money around, Clare was quite certain there was no way Mitch would be able to find the true destinations of the line of credit proceeds. She chuckled to herself as she visualized Mitch finding out about the funds and desperately trying to find the precious money.

CHAPTER 17

BRANDON, or whatever his real name was, called Sheriff Buford Blakeley early Sunday morning and was ready to meet again. Only this time he wanted Ernie Lambert to be included in the meeting. Brandon caught Buford as he was having his Sunday morning breakfast at Ruby's. For this reason Buford couldn't say much as he was presiding at the board of directors' table at Ruby's. Brandon knew Buford was having breakfast with his buddies when he called. He wisely realized this would keep the conversation to a minimum and Buford would quickly agree to Brandon's meeting preferences.

Brandon had waited twenty-four hours more than he had earlier promised to contact Blakeley. This had worried Buford so much that he had trouble sleeping the night before. The thought that kept going through his mind was, "What if someone had followed Brandon and intimidated him into silence, or worse?"

After a quick call to Ernie Lambert, as Ernie was leaving his home for church services, Buford had the meeting with Brandon set. They would meet him at a remote campground in Roaring River State Park at 8:00 p.m. that evening. For the rest of the day, Buford Blakeley was as nervous as a groom on his wedding day. The plan was to sit down with Ernie at Ernie's office at 6:30 p.m., prepare their questions for Brandon, and then drive to the park and hope and pray that Brandon would show as promised.

Per their plan, Ernie and Buford made it to the set meeting location around 7:55 p.m. They drove to the park using a back route as Brandon had instructed. This way anyone trying to follow them could be easily spotted by an alert eye. At around 8:05 p.m., Brandon appeared. Neither Ernie nor Buford could figure out how Brandon could appear without being noticed, but Buford was so glad to see him he nearly gave Brandon a hug, but was able to restrain himself. The young man shook hands with Ernie and Buford and they made their way to a remote cabin that appeared to have been unused the entire summer. Ernie decided to take a more firm approach with Brandon. He wanted to make sure he and Buford weren't being led down a trap being laid by Mitch McMasters.

Ernie immediately got to business, "So Brandon, Buford has told me an interesting story about your discussion on Friday. What you have to say tonight better be good. To drag Buford and me out on a Sunday night better be worth it."

Brandon smiled before he replied. It appeared he liked Ernie's direct style. "Sir, if I were you, I would be pissed off as well if I were dragged out on a Sunday night for a wild goose chase. But I can assure you that you will not be disappointed with what I have to say. You must promise to keep me protected, because there will be repercussions if word of my talks with you guys gets out."

Buford motioned to Ernie to take the lead in the discussion. "Brandon, we will not let this out, but we have to know everything in order to protect you. If you leave something out, it could be the one thing needed to protect you. Do you understand?"

"I clearly understand. You better not hang me out to dry."

"We will not. But you already know that. Otherwise, you wouldn't have contacted us in the first place."

Brandon offered no reply. He sat on a wooden chair for a moment and then be began to explain what he had observed recently.

"Ok, let me start with Haley, and it should lead into other directions. I've known Haley for a long time. We were friends in school. I have also been a friend for a long time with Chad McMasters. We graduated from Bouvier together. Chad headed to Mizzou, and I started working here at the park and doing various odd jobs. I have been taking some classes at the community college in town. During the past year while Chad was at Mizzou, he asked me to keep an eye on Haley. Since she was so hot, Chad was afraid that there would be a lot of guys trying to hit on her. Surprisingly, that wasn't the case. It seemed like most of the guys in town were intimidated to approach Haley, either because of her looks or because she was dating a McMasters. Then, when they bought her the convertible, nobody would go near her. It was during this time period that Haley and I started hanging out. She knew Chad had put me on her tail, so to speak. So she said she would make my surveillance job easier by running around with me. Since I work evenings here in the park, it was pretty easy for us to hang out without anyone seeing us. After Chad left for Italy, the relationship between Haley and me changed. It became a sexual relationship. I will spare you two the details, but I can definitely see why Chad wanted Haley to have that nice car. After a month into our relationship, Haley dropped me. She never said anything; she just stopped coming down to the park and wouldn't return my phone calls. If we had been in a fight or something I would have understood, but things were going great and then she just vanished from our relationship.

I have to admit, I'm nineteen years old; and I was in love with Haley Fulz. I fell hard for her. I couldn't understand what had happened, so I started doing some snooping."

Buford and Ernie were thoroughly engrossed in Brandon's tale. At this point Ernie was patiently waiting for the next direction of Brandon's episode, "What do you mean you started snooping, Brandon?"

"Ok, you have to promise not to get me fired?"

Ernie hated this question, but he moved forward, "Ok, Brandon, as long as you haven't done anything illegal."

"Well, it's probably not illegal; but it's not right either. Let's just say, since I work nights here at the park, I have lots of free unsupervised time on my job. I started following Haley, and I soon discovered that she had dumped me for none other than Chad's dad. That's right, she was screwing Mitch McMasters. For a while she was with him almost every night. So every night I would finish my work list and sneak down to good ole Mitch's cabin to see if Haley was there. It's only a few minutes from where I work in the park. I could be back at work and nobody ever noticed. I know I shouldn't have, but I was in love, hurt, and basically became kind of a stalker. But for you guys that's probably a good thing."

Ernie immediately shot back, "Why would that be a good thing, Brandon?"

"Because I was down there the night she died. I got there about ten minutes before Haley left Mitch's house. All I know is I heard Haley yelling at Mitch and she jumped into her car and Mitch took off after her. I pulled in behind Mitch's Jeep, but I kept my distance so he wouldn't see my vehicle. They were driving like a couple of race car drivers. I was having a hard time keeping up. The next thing I know is I saw Mitch's brake lights light up and then I heard a crash of some sort.

I slowed down so I wouldn't get involved in whatever had happened. By the time I came through, both cars were gone. I didn't really know exactly what had happened until I started hearing the police and ambulance sirens. That's when I knew for sure that there had been a wreck and how bad it was."

Ernie inquired, "Did you ever see Mitch's Jeep after the crash?"

Brandon paused and looked around before he answered. "I didn't, but I know someone who did. that's where things get sticky because it involves Willie."

WILLIE STILLWAGON, a Bouvier native, had been a decorated Vietnam veteran who got hooked on various drugs during his two stints in the war. Basically, he fried most of his mind on acid and other drugs before he could arrive back from Vietnam in the fall of 1970. The army immediately discharged Willie, and from there he led a sad life of alcohol and drugs for several years before he came back home to Bouvier. His family got him cleaned up at a couple of rehab units, and his attorney obtained for a full military disability. Even though the government had concluded that his mind could not function in a normal job capacity, it still worked in many other valuable ways for Willie. For a while his monthly disability check and doing various odd jobs kept Willie happy, occupied, and basically out of trouble. But it was only temporarily.

Willie Stillwagon eventually migrated back to the life of drugs. But he did so in a discreet manner. Standing hunchbacked, which made his five foot eight inch body frame appear even smaller, most people in Bouvier thought Willie as being a bit crazy, but harmless. He just wandered around town most days, especially during the winter when there were no yards to mow or weeds to be cut.

The meth trade was growing rapidly in the Bouvier area as the remote landscape provided an opportune place to secretly produce the highly addictive drug. Willie, who had the free time and the experience in the drug culture moved, into the Bouvier meth culture. At first, Willie did so as a dealer, not as a user. His family had been successful in getting him cleaned and free of the desires to use drugs. Willie however, wasn't rid of the desire to make lots of money from the meth trade.

Willie Stillwagon's mode of operation for his promising meth distribution business was a bit odd, but enormously successful. Most days, Willie, posing as a homeless veteran, would line up his drug sales as he stood near the entrance of Roaring River State Park. Being homeless was one claim that Willie could honestly make. But in Willie's case, his homeless situation was by choice, not by necessity or circumstances. Willie would stand for hours on end enticing out of town tourists out of cash. The donations would bring in at least two grand a month for Willie, all tax free. He also would use this as an opportunity to communicate with potential meth clients through coded gestures about their future hook ups to exchange cash for drugs.

Amazingly, Willie was able to pull all of this off while also serving as a snitch for the local law enforcement officers. Sheriff Buford Blakeley and his crew had known Willie Stillwagon from their high school days. They all knew that Willie was a bit crazy, but he was a lovable character as well. Deep down, they felt sorry for Willie for coming back from Vietnam with a mind as messed up as a box full of clothes hangers. For that reason and one other, they didn't hassle Willie for prying cash from the unsuspecting tourists as he did his homeless Vet routine. The other reason was that Willie became a valuable intelligence source for Sheriff Blakeley. Each and every day, Willie would peek inside the cars of thousands of people as they entered the popular Roaring River State Park. And each day Willie saw things that people had hoped to stay hidden. Willie's information helped Sheriff Blakeley solve burglary cases, missing children alerts, and track down drunk drivers. One time, he even helped them locate an armed bank robber. However, until their meeting with Brandon, Sheriff never knew Willie was involved in the county's meth trade. For his valuable information, Willie received around $1,000 each month in cash from the Sheriff's department for his covert operation. The month he helped nab the bank robber, Willie netted $10,000 for his assistance. The local bank had no idea their cash had made its way into the pockets of Willie Stillwagon.

Ernie Lambert and Buford Blakeley immediately came to attention when Brandon brought up Willie's name in connection with Mitch McMasters.

Buford inquired, "You mean Willie Stillwagon saw Mitch McMasters the night of the wreck?"

"Yes, Willie had just finished his homeless routine that evening and had made his way down the hill to the main fishing area of the park. It was there that he saw Mitch and the Jeep with a rather large hole in the right front fender."

"How do you know Willie saw Mitch that night?"

"Because he told me that evening."

"Why would Willie tell you about this?"

"Willie's a friend. Since I work nights at the park, I have come to know Willie quite well."

Due to some things Brandon had said in their first meeting, Buford sensed Brandon had more to reveal, so he pressed further. "Earlier you said it would get sticky because it involves Willie. What did you mean by that?"

"This is where I need your absolute promise that you can protect me. Otherwise, I will shut my damn mouth and let you guys figure this out on your own."

Ernie leaned forward and looked Brandon straight in the eye, "Son, if you have something to say then say it. Because you have our word that we will keep you totally safe. What or whom are you afraid of?"

Brandon's composure began to change. He started walking around the cabin and peering out each window as if he were being hunted. After a few moments, Brandon appeared to calm down. "Maybe I need an attorney because I'm not real comfortable talking about all of this right now."

Ernie feared Brandon would shut down the meeting and never show up again. For that reason he was prepared to offer almost anything at his disposal to keep Brandon there and talking. "Brandon, what can we do to ease your concerns?"

"Keep me alive and out of jail. That's the promise I need from you."

"Ok, just a minute, Brandon. Have you committed any crimes in connection with Willie Stillwagon?"

"Yes!"

"Were these crimes violent or non violent crimes?"

"Non violent."

"Were you a leader or a follower in the crimes?"

"Definitely a follower."

"Have these crimes placed you in danger?"

"Not any type of imminent danger. But it has put me in contact with people who are no Sunday school teachers, if you get my drift."

"Why do you want to discuss crimes you've committed with two law enforcement officers?"

"I think it's my only way to get out of this mess alive. I know too much." At this point Brandon broke down and began to sob. The confident, even somewhat cocky side of Brandon was long gone. With his head buried in his hands, both Ernie Lambert and Buford Blakeley knew they had the real deal with Brandon. He was a smart kid who had made some bad decisions and now was his sole opportunity to escape unharmed.

Ernie Lambert walked over to Brandon and put his arm on his shoulder. "Brandon, if everything you tell us is true, we will work it out so that you are protected and you don't go to jail. But if you lead us down the wrong path, the get out of jail free card will go out the window. Do you understand?"

Between sobs Brandon mumbled, "Yes, I do."

ERNIE and Buford allowed Brandon to collect himself before they began to pull more information from their star witness to whatever crimes he had committed. Ernie began the examination. "Brandon, tell us the types of activities you have participated in and have witnessed and why you feel like you are in jeopardy."

"Let me make this clear; Willie isn't the one who scares me. His partner does."

Ernie inquired, "Who's his partner and why does he scare you? Tell me what types of activities that Willie and his partner have been engaged in."

"I told Buford a couple of days ago that one of his staff is on the take with the local meth dealers, among others. Well, this guy is Alex Vander or A.V. as everyone calls him. If A.V.

finds out I am talking, I am dead. There is no other way around it."

"How is A.V. tied to Willie Stillwagon and what is their scheme?"

"Willie has some meth labs on some rough land near the lake. Plus, he knows who runs all of the other meth labs in the area. Willie shakes down the meth lab guys for protection money. If they pay, they get to continue to play the meth game. If they don't pay, well A.V. and his department come in and shut down the meth lab. And then Buford gets his picture in the paper after the arrest. Willie and A.V. are making a killing off the meth industry in the county."

"Do you know of any other law enforcement guys involved with A.V?"

"Willie has indicated that A.V. doesn't trust anyone else, and he doesn't want to share any of his meth earnings with other deputies."

Ernie shot a glare at Buford. He was thinking, 'How in the hell could you not know this was going on?' But Ernie also felt responsible because he knew nothing as well.

Ernie continued, "Ok, where do you fit in and have you actually witnessed any of this going down?"

"For the past six months I have been a mule for Willie."

"What is a mule, Brandon?"

"Willie sends me out to pick up the cash from the meth lab owner who agrees to the pay to play game. I have also made meth drops for Willie and collected the cash for those transactions."

"How long to protection payment last?"

"It lasts as long as A.V. says it lasts. The way it works is, the meth lab owner pays Willie and A.V. to stay in business. Then in about nine months, A.V. comes to Willie and says the state is going to start another big crack down on drugs in the county, especially meth. It's then that the meth guys have to pay again to stay in business. Some get pissed and decide to tell Willie to stick it. And guess what, they get nailed by A.V. The beauty of it all is that A.V. is never known to the meth guy as the one who is shaking them down. A couple of meth producers have threatened Willie. But deep down they are afraid of Willie because they know someone with some real muscle is behind him. They fear messing with him and possibly risk getting shut down for good."

"So you have worked solely with Willie and have never been in contact with A.V? How do you know A.V. is involved as the mastermind of the scheme?"

"A lot of stuff happens right here in the park at night. From my perch I see most of it. Over time, Willie and I became friends. Eventually, he became to trust me. I was broke, and he offered me a way to make some extra money as his mule. As time went on, I began to watch Willie and A.V. meeting up in the park, in the dark of night. No one knew I was watching. The more I became friends with Willie, the more he began to discuss his operation."

"So Willie has told you, point blank, that A.V. is involved in the meth operation."

"You're damn right he has. One night he had a big wad of cash in his pocket. He pulled it out and started laughing like a mad man, which many think Willie is. He then proceeded to really let loose about how he and A.V. were screwing over all the meth pushers. He thinks it rather comical that a deranged Vietnam vet could be pulling down over two hundred grand a year, tax free, while posing as a homeless derelict. He would laugh and say, 'Only in America. Thank God for the war on drugs'"

Ernie and Buford just sat there for a moment saying nothing. The fact that a guy posing as a mindless, homeless Vietnam vet was making a fool of their law enforcement efforts was not a laughing matter to either party. To accent his point Brandon handed over his cell phone to Ernie and Buford. After hitting the play button, they sat in disbelief as they witnessed Brandon's conversation with Willie, as Willie discussed A.V.'s scheme to shake down the meth dealers. Brandon had, in fact, saved the best for last. There they had his whole story summarized on a video tape, as the county's biggest meth dealer discussed his whole mode of operation. In Ernie Lambert's mind, there was only one word to describe the video, '*priceless.*'

Their meeting with Brandon concluded shortly before midnight. Just before it ended, they cleared up Brandon's real name. He was actually Brad Ellsworth. Ernie asked if Brandon really existed and Brad replied, "Yeah, Brandon is real. He comes and goes. I never really know when he will be here or when he will leave. But yes he really exists." Ernie wanted more, "What's Brandon's name and what does he do for a living?"

"His name is Brandon Farve. He is twenty-five years old and he used to work with me at the park. But Willie put him to work and it was too lucrative. Now he works as a mule for Willie and the rest of the time I have no idea where he goes. I do know he likes to gamble and fish. He takes Willie's toughest jobs, if you know what I mean."

Ernie saw the real Brandon as yet another way to neatly tie things up for Willie. "Ok, here's the deal, Brad. When the real Brandon gets to town, you have to let us know ASAP. He has to be in the deal, since he knows so much. Otherwise, he could be in danger when our prosecution comes tumbling down. You understand, Brad?"

Brad silently nodded. He keenly understood the stakes would be very high when Ernie and Buford started arresting the county's most notorious dope dealers.

Ernie and Buford had learned so much during the past four hours that their heads were spinning. They had far surpassed their primary objective, forming a trust with Brandon, now known as Brad. A plan was put in place where Brad Ellsworth could be in contact with Ernie or Buford at a moment's notice.

Unbeknownst to Brad, Ernie planned to contact the U.S. Attorney's office to obtain special protection for him. The fact that he held the key to bringing down possibly one of the biggest meth cartels in the nation would definitely get the feds attention. In addition, helping bring murder charges for the most powerful man in the country, would assist in the bargaining. Buford and Ernie acutely knew they couldn't trust anyone else on the Sheriff's department to help with the investigation. No telling how many men on the force were leaking information to Alex Vander. The feds were their only answer.

Both headed home filled with as much adrenaline as a couple of teenage boys on the night of their opening football game. Only this game was for keeps for so many people and for so many reasons.

CHAPTER 18

AS was his custom in similar circumstances, the first person that Ernie Lambert called on Monday morning was the esteemed Barry County circuit judge, Altus T. Claibourn. Ernie reached out to Judge Claibourn for many reasons. The primary reason was to prep him for potential search warrants that would be needed if the meth lab investigation proceeded as Ernie expected. However, the secondary and probably most important reason was Judge Claibourn was the one person that Ernie could talk to when faced with a delicate and confidential matter. Ernie knew that when Judge Altus T. Claibourn said he would keep a conversation secret, he meant it. A vow of confidentiality was a sacred vow in the eyes of Judge Claibourn. Additionally, Ernie greatly valued the judge's ability to analyze a complex situation down to a set of clear and understandable basic facts.

The judge was hungry and jumped at the chance of breakfast with Ernie Lambert. They didn't want to be seen having breakfast together as it would raise too many noisy questions, so the judge sent a clerk to Ruby's for a couple of orders of Ruby's incredible biscuits and gravy. They would eat and discuss matters in the judge's private office, located on the third floor of the Barry County Courthouse. Ernie Lambert and the food arrived almost at the same exact time. Judge Claibourn was pacing his office, which was the norm, when waiting on good food and even better gossip.

Judge Claibourn was in his late sixties. He stood five feet eleven inches tall and about one hundred and seventy five pounds. A trim and very handsome man., he grew his gray hair somewhat long and combed it straight back. Altus Claibourn gave the appearance of an eccentric college professor. But he still possessed one of the keenest legal minds of the circuit judges in the state of Missouri. He had originally planned to retire when he reached the age of sixty, but those plans went out the window because his wife was one of the counties biggest spenders and he knew that retirement was a recipe for bankruptcy. But the real reason was that he loved the job too much.

While they ate, Ernie entertained Judge Claibourn with a summary of the meeting the night before with Brandon, now known as Brad Ellsworth. After Ernie was finished, Judge Claibourn looked up at Ernie, with his reading glasses perched on the end of his nose and asked, "Let me get this straight, Ernie, you are going to bring down the most powerful man in the county for murder and at the same time prosecute one of the biggest meth rings in the nation, while busting a rouge cop? What are you going to do next week after you get all of this accomplished?"

Both shared a good laugh at the judge's assessment of the information. The judge then became very serious and walked over to Ernie, "Listen son, I am proud you have the guts and determination to go after this, but keep this in mind. If this isn't handled with exquisite care, you stand the risk of getting a bunch of people killed. And you and Buford could be included. I am sure you have thought all this through, but please do it right."

"Judge, I completely understand your concerns. The thought of all of this hinging on the testimony of Willie

Stillwagon makes me nervous as hell. Everyone, including the United States military, thinks he's a nutcase. Will a jury ever buy into Willie being able to pull all this off?"

"Two things will seal it: Alex Vander being the real mastermind and Willie being the puppet. The other thing is the money. Where the hell is Willie keeping all this money he's supposedly making off the government, the Sheriff's department, the unsuspecting tourists, and the meth dealers?"

"Buford and I suspect that his brother's construction company is a scam to launder the drug money. The brother's big ass house with the fancy iron gate most likely was paid for by Willie. I figure that when we start nosing around in his brother's financial affairs we will find that almost all of his supposed construction company customers pay him with cold hard cash. I bet we won't find many checks being deposited into the business account. It will be nearly all cash."

Judge Claibourn could see that Ernie Lambert had thought through all of the potential pitfalls which could arise in the pursuit of such a dangerous, high profile case. He assured Ernie that he would have no problem issuing search warrants, if needed. The one part of the case that concerned Claibourn the most wasn't Mitch McMasters, but rather Alex Vander. The judge wasn't as confident as Ernie and Buford that Vander was working alone in his kickback scheme. The judge was concerned that Buford might have one or two trusted deputies working along with Vander. If that were the case, Judge Claibourn was concerned that these guys would do anything, including kill, to protect their little gold mine, not to mention avoiding a potential life in prison, if caught. Despite his confidence in Ernie Lambert, Judge Claibourn felt much better knowing that Ernie and Buford would be assisted by undercover agents with the U.S. Marshall's office, who specialized in drug and corruption cases.

After they finished their breakfast, Ernie Lambert eagerly made his way to his office. He hadn't been this enthused to get to work in a long time. Once he had left his office, Judge Altus T. Claibourn quietly said a prayer for his friend. He knew Ernie's career and possibly his life hinged on the success of the investigation.

SHERIFF Buford Blakeley was chosen to approach Willie Stillwagon for several reasons. The primary and most obvious was that they had been long-time friends and Buford was the one who had set up the information sharing operation with Willie. Willie and Buford had developed a mutual trust for each other. The fact that Willie had decided to betray that trust was greatly unsettling to Buford. After a stern lecture from Ernie Lambert, Buford clearly saw the need not to let his personal feelings of betrayal impact the most important criminal investigation in recent history of Barry County. Buford felt as if he had been played for a fool by both Willie Stillwagaon and Alex Vander, but Ernie assured Buford that he supported him one hundred percent. Ernie reminded Buford that corruption happens all the time, regardless of the size of the operation, whether it's a business or a major corporation. You could make a zillion more laws and regulations, but they would never take away the human desire of greed. Some handle it better than others, but it's always lurking around the corner. Clearly, Alex Vander and Willie Stillwagon set the curve for their inability to handle their desire for money and the shortcuts they would take to obtain it as fast as possible.

Per the plan put in place by Ernie, Buford, and the federal agents, Buford picked up Willie just as he was setting up for a day of panhandling and fleecing of the unsuspecting tourists entering the state park. Willie wasn't initially surprised by Buford's offer for a ride. Since he was one of Buford's informants, they interacted quite often. Earlier that morning, Willie had been caught on a surveillance recording setting up a meth drop with Brad Ellsworth. According to the federal agents assisting Buford, the detail that Brad elicited from Willie was priceless. He even got Willie to discuss his most recent bribe, which he paid to Alex Vander. Ernie, Buford, and the boys with the feds were ready to swoop in on Willie Stillwagon.

It was an unusually hot September morning when Willie jumped into Buford's unmarked police cruiser. As was his custom, Willie had not bathed in several days; and this morning he was especially ripe. He smelled so bad, Buford nearly gagged when Willie sat down in the vehicle. Willie informed Buford that he didn't have any leads for him that day. According to Willie, things had been slow recently. Willie had discerned that the economy must have people staying at home and mostly out of trouble. Buford had a terrible time not smarting back to Willie about him being a lying, backstabbing, ingrate; but he let his professional manner override his emotions. It was difficult, however.

Willie seemed totally unconcerned when Buford pulled into a secluded lake home that the feds had rented from a retired couple, who spent their summers in Montana. It would serve as their investigation headquarters for the time being. Before he knew what had happened, Willie was being escorted into the den of the lake home by Buford and two federal agents, who appeared very stern and basically pissed off that they were having to touch a guy who smelled like hot urine.

As the uptight and arrogant federal agents worked with the placement of Willie in the desired chair, Ernie snickered and thought to himself, 'Boys, welcome to Barry County.'

The start of the interrogation of Willie Stillwagon did not go as the federal agents had expected or hoped. First, they had to get accustomed to Willie's horrible aroma. There are people who smell bad, and then there is Willie. Next, was the fact that Willie spoke in what they soon began to describe as Willie words. Willie mumbled a lot; and when he did speak, it was in spurts. Once he became comfortable with someone, he would speak in a much clearer and smoother fashion. Clearly, Willie was not comfortable with the federal agents, and they were having one hell of a time trying to understand him. After an hour Buford was able to get Willie calmed down, and he begun to grasp his situation.

The feds had done their homework on Willie. His military files showed Willie to be someone who was fearful of the structure of the United States armed forces. The files also showed that Willie had suffered a nervous breakdown in Vietnam. According to his military doctors, that had more to do with his behavior and anti-social tendencies than his drug usage. Knowing this, the feds used the threat of having to go back to the military as a weapon of fear. That did more to motivate Willie into cooperating in their investigation. After a couple of hours, Willie was compliant with the feds demands. He discussed in great detail the meth operation he and Alex Vander controlled.

Once they got Willie on board to cooperate, in exchange for some very lenient treatment by Ernie and the feds, which would more than likely include a move to the federal witness protection program, they advanced to the issue of Haley's wreck. Surprisingly, Willie vividly remembered the night of the wreck. He volunteered that he was in the park when the wreck happened. When asked if he had seen any vehicles that night that might have appeared to have been in a fender bender, Willie's response stunned everyone.

"Yeah, I saw that damn Mitch McMaster drive up with his Jeep's front light all bashed in. He stumbled out of the Jeep and walked over to the pay phone and made a call. He put a rag over the phone while he made the call. I snuck behind him and heard him report a car wreck. It wasn't long after that when I heard the ambulances come flying down to the park. I had heard a crash of some type before that effing Mitch McMasters drove up. You want to see the little picture I took of Mitchie at the pay phone?"

When Willie asked that question, one of the feds accidentally blurted out, "Holy shit!"

Willie Stillwagon proceeded to pull out his cell phone and from it he produced a photo dated September 1. The image was vintage Mitch McMasters, wearing his orange visor, his hair messed up, red faced, and appearing scared. Willie's photo even picked up the Jeep in the background. The gash in the front right fender was barely visible, but it was still there.

As he reviewed the damning photo, Buford Blakeley had the urge to hug his old friend, Willie, but Willie's stench was too much and Buford resorted to a simple wink, which silently said, "Thanks, old friend."

Willie gave Buford a nod back. Willie knew he had screwed over his good friend, Buford Blakeley, but deep down he knew the photo of Mitch McMasters had gone a long way to help repay Buford for the harm he had done. Now, he had one more very important thing to do to further assist his old friend.

The plan to get Alex Vander discussing the meth scheme on a surveillance video would be easier said than done. There were many obstacles to getting it done. Namely, getting Willie Stillwagon to follow a script was the most daunting challenge facing Sheriff Blakeley and the federal agents. Amazingly, Willie agreed to attempt the operation, without much objection. Blakeley correctly assumed that Willie still held some loyalty to him and felt bad for breaking the trust he had placed in Willie. If Willie could get Alex to talk about what the feds wanted him to say, Willie knew it would greatly help out his old friend. Willie also understood the danger involved in an operation of this type. If Alex Vander discovered that Willie was in possession of recording devices, there was a strong chance that Willie's life could be in danger. As much as they could, the federal agents discussed various code words that Willie could use if the meeting with Vander started going in a bad direction. The frustrating part for the feds was getting Willie to remember the code words. Some parts of Willie's mind worked normally and other parts had difficulty with basic functions. Having to recite to memory code words was definitely one of the things that Willie's mind did not handle well.

The federal agents rehearsed with Willie to the point where they felt reasonably confident in his ability to handle the session with Alex Vander. The thing they feared most was Willie getting so nervous that he would piss his pants. With his personality, it was a distinct possibility that this could happen. The plan was to have Willie call Vander set up a time and place to discuss their operation; and get everything, including Vander's incriminating words on surveillance tape. The usual meeting spot would be prepped with hidden microphones and cameras. If everything worked according to their plan, in the next twenty-four to forty-eight hours they would have their case against Alex Vander sealed shut.

Buford drove Willie near his usual post, at the entrance of Roaring River State Park, and Willie resumed his daily activities of fleecing unsuspecting tourists. As he drove away, Buford hoped his old friend would be up to the task ahead. If he could successfully pull it off, it would help Buford make one of the biggest drug busts in the history of the state. But it still hinged on none other than Willie Stillwagon. Buford knew he probably wouldn't sleep a wink as he would be worried about Willie's command performance. The exact time would depend upon when Willie could corral Alex Vander into the precisely prepared noose being set up by the federal boys.

CHAPTER 19

MITCH McMASTERS was soon learning the hard part of keeping people happy and content when they discover you are desperate and will pay cold hard cash to keep their mouth's shut. Mitch was living the old saying, "There is not honor among thieves." The past couple of days for Mitch had been spent trying to make all of the various parties, who had been paid handsome sums of cash, satisfied with their recent gravy trains, courtesy of good time Mitch.

Rufus Jones had found a new bass boat that would really help him with his two beloved passions, bass fishing and beer drinking. The price tag for the boat that Rufus desired was $54,271. Mitch tried to explain to Rufus that he could not afford to purchase that kind of boat for him; they had agreed to $5,000 per month. Rufus wasn't taking no for an answer. He could smell through Mitch's desperate air that he possessed some really important goods on Mitch. And Rufus knew well enough that he had better strike while the iron was hot. He knew once whatever Mitch was really hiding from blew over, his information wouldn't be as valuable. Consequently, he was going to ride this horse as hard and as fast as he could, so to speak.

The next crisis Mitch had to deal with was Pate Johnston. Pate had contacted Mitch and informed him that the cost of living in Destin was going to be much more than he could ever imagine and there was no way he could immediately find work that paid worth a damn. He too had found a boat that he couldn't live without. Pate's demand was for another $50,000 and an additional $75,478 for the boat. But as Pate, arrogantly put it, "You should be happy I found a bargain. Most of the boats are running $125,000 to $200,000." Despite Pate's insistence, it did little to perk up Mitch's spirits, which were about low as they could get.

The combined total of Rufus and Pate's demands was $179,749, not to mention the supply of beer, accessories, and bass tournament entrance fees that Rufus would more than likely request along with the new boat. Mitch was beside himself over how he could handle the escalating demands. All of the previous pay offs to Rufus, Pate Johnston, and Morgan Langley's parents had nearly depleted his family trust account. If he was going to continue to keep everyone happy and quiet, he would have to find the money and find it fast.

Reluctantly, Mitch realized the only way for him to keep the cash train rolling down the tracks was to tap into the newspaper's million dollar line of credit at the Bouvier Community Bank. Mitch hated to do so in more ways than he could possibly imagine. The primary reasons were that a sizable advance would get the attention of the lending officer, who happened to be the bank president, Carter Franklin. Mitch was not a big fan of Franklin. He saw him as a whiny, gutless, fence sitter, who could not keep confidences. Mitch feared Carter whispering of the loan advance to some of his buddies and then it spreading in no telling what direction. However, Carter also kissed Mitch's ass whenever he called, which was something Mitch loved, even if he wouldn't admit it. The other concern was the possibility of Clare finding out about the draws on the credit line. Since she was technically the corporation president, she would get any interest billing on the loan when there was money advanced on it. From Mitch's recollection, it had been years since the line of credit had been used. Eventually, Mitch resolved himself to the fact that this was his only way out of his mess. He would just make sure to get any interest billings mailed to his lake house address, to avoid any messy discussions with Clare about why he needed $179,749 drawn from the newspaper's line of credit. After pacing around the lake cabin for over an hour, Mitch found the courage to make to call to Carter Franklin. He hated doing So but he had no other alternatives. As he made the call, he thought to himself, "Why did I put myself in this position, why?"

Carter Franklin's secretary, Alex Chambers, a perky young bank employee, took the call for Carter. When Alex realized she had Mitch McMasters on the phone, she got both excited and nervous. Alex Chambers, like several women in Bouvier, was smitten by Mitch's good looks, the aura of the McMasters' prestige, and the successful way he carried himself. Whenever Mitch would come into the Bouvier Community Bank, Alex would try to find a reason to get Mitch's attention or ask him a question about one of his accounts. Today, she was taken aback by the abrupt and rude manner from Mitch. He wasn't his normal flirtatious self.

When Carter Franklin heard Alex say the name, Mitch McMasters, he immediately broke out in a cold sweat. All weekend long he had worried about the million dollar loan advance he had authorized for Clare McMasters. Even though Clare was legally authorized to make the transaction, Carter Franklin was deeply worried about what would happen when Mitch found out about the advance. Now, he was about to face the dreaded conversation with Mitch McMasters.

Carter was nervous and sweating bullets. He answered the phone in his usual, over the top, nauseatingly friendly manner. But due to his nervousness, it was so over the top and fake that even a self absorbed guy like Mitch McMasters could see through Carter Franklin's plastic persona.

"Mitch, great to hear from you, I'm surprised to hear your voice. I figured you would be on the back nine, taking some serious cash from your golf buddies. What can I do for you on this gorgeous day?"

Mitch was in no mood for Carter's usual banter. He avoided any pretense of conversation and went straight to business.

"Hey, listen, Carter, advance $200,000 from the credit line into my business account, you know, the one in my name." When Carter heard Mitch utter his command, he froze for a moment not knowing what to say or do. He knew that he was not emotionally equipped to handle a confrontation with Mitch McMasters.

"Well, uh, Mitch, let's see here. Uh, let me pull the account up. All day I have been having trouble with my computer. Well, uh, man, I'm sorry about this; but I can't get the line pulled up right now, Mitch. Uh, can I call you back in a few minutes once our computers come back on line?" Carter hoped the computer line would allow him some time to get his thoughts together for what to tell Mitch. All he could think about at the moment was, "Please don't yell at me, Mitch. I only did what I was told to do."

Unfortunately for Carter, the computer line wasn't working on Mitch. A clearly annoyed Mitch McMasters yelled, "Dammit, Carter, just do the advance. The line has a million available. Just move $200,000 into my business account. Make sure you put it in the account that is in my name only. Got it, Carter?"

Carter was fast realizing he was going to have to deliver some bad news before things got out of hand with Mitch. If he didn't speak up fast, Mitch was going to conclude the conversation and start writing checks on the account, thinking he had a fresh $200,000 to blow. The thought of Mitch McMasters writing hot checks, based upon an assumed deposit into his account, gave Carter the courage he desperately needed at the moment.

"Uh, listen, Mitch; before you hang up, I need to tell you something about the credit line."

A perturbed Mitch McMasters was taken aback by Carter's statement and the nervous tenor in his voice.

"What do you mean; you need to tell me something about the credit line, Carter?"

"Well, Mitch, uh, at the moment, there isn't any credit available on the line."

A red faced Mitch McMasters couldn't believe what he had just been told.

"What the hell do you mean there isn't any credit available on the line? That line is set up for a million damn dollars. So I suggest you get you ass in gear and get me my money real quick. I can't believe this shit. What kind of bank are you running, Carter? Get your damn computers straightened out, or I will move my business somewhere else."

"Uh, Mitch, it isn't a computer error with your account. There simply isn't any money available on your line, at this time. It has been maxed out."

"You know, Carter, this is bull shit. There is a computer mix up, and it's really pissing me off. You of all people should know we have a million dollars sitting available on the line. Hell, we haven't used the damn line in over five or ten years."

"Mitch, the line was advanced to the hilt on Saturday. Maybe you should talk to your wife about this matter."

Mitch started to say something, but then he realized that he couldn't talk. Whether he was having a stroke or a severe panic attack, it didn't matter. Mitch thought he was actually dying. The phone line went silent long enough that poor ole Carter became concerned as he asked, "Mitch, are you still there? Mitch, Mitch?"

When he finally caught his breath, Mitch McMasters came back with a fury. He furiously shot back at Carter Franklin. "Why the hell did you let her advance all that money? You had no damn right to do that without my authorization."

Franklin weakly replied, "Mitch, she is president and secretary of the corporation. We were just following the corporate authorization." Before Franklin could finish his sentence, Mitch interrupted Franklin and continued his tirade.

"I don't give a damn what your documents say. The documents I am looking at right now say that I am the owner of the damn corporation you just advanced a million bucks on without my signature, approval, or consent. I am Mitch McMasters. My family has owned this newspaper for longer than you will ever know, and you think you can mess with my business credit line without talking to me first? You advanced a million bucks without my authorization. I own the damn newspaper, don't you know that?"

"Uh, well, Mitch, the documents state clearly that…"

"I don't want to hear about your supposed documents. Apparently, you don't' know what the hell you are doing. So I am going to give you clear and precise instructions, so listen up. Reverse the million dollar advance in the next thirty minutes and then do the $200,000 advance that I just requested. Otherwise, I will have your ass fired and will be suing your little bank for a million bucks, plus damages. Carter, are we clear on what you are to do?"

A terrified Carter Franklin knew he was in way too far over his head. Deep down, Franklin knew that a candy assed wimp weasel, like himself, should never deal with guys like Mitch McMasters. The only thing that kept him from crying like a baby was the fact that the curtains to his office, which faced the main lobby of the bank, were wide open. Crying in front of his staff and a lobby full of customers wasn't an option for the weak willed Franklin. Deep down Carter wanted to just give Mitch his $200,000, which would stop the abusive yelling. Carter was at least smart enough on this occasion not to go with the expedient route. Namely, because he knew he would go to jail for bank fraud, among other crimes that would be committed in an effort to keep Mitch happy. So Carter took a deep breath and stood his ground against the powerful Mitch McMasters.

With his voice quivering lightly, Carter replied, "Mitch, as much as I would like to accommodate your request, I have no legal basis to do so. I would suggest that you speak with Clare about the advance she did. Apparently, there has been a misunderstanding between the two of you regarding who is the authorized party for the newspaper's corporation affairs. Would you like for me to get Clare on the phone to discuss this?"

The mention of Clare's name verbally hit Mitch right in the gut. Discussing his attempted $200,000 advance from the newspaper's line of credit with Clare McMasters was the last thing Mitch wanted to do. Mitch decided to end this nightmare of a conversation before it got any worse for him.

"Listen, Carter, I don't need you telling me what to do. I own the damn newspaper and I suggest you reread your corporation papers very clearly. When you get finished, you will realize you just cost your bank a million bucks. So do as I have clearly instructed and everything will be fine. I will expect the $200,000 to be in my account in the next thirty minutes."

Before Carter could respond, Mitch McMasters had hung up. Carter Franklin was a nervous wreck. He wondered to himself, 'Did Clare really have the proper authorization to advance the money from the newspaper's line of credit? And did I really read the corporation documents before I did the advance for Clare?' The next thing the staff and customers of the Bouvier Community Bank saw was the image of Carter Franklin running to the bank's file room. There he found the loan file for the *Bouvier Gazette* and immediately began reading the corporation documents. After five minutes Carter Franklin found what he hoped would save his job and the bank's reputation and legal standing, not to mention a million bucks, plus damages. To be sure, he placed a call to the bank's attorney, Raleigh J. Calhoun.

Carter Franklin was able to reach Raleigh at his office. As Carter began to explain everything that had transpired with Mitch McMasters, Raleigh could hardly contain himself. He nearly started laughing out loud at the thought of Mitch finding out that Clare had drained the newspaper's line of credit. He could visualize a red faced, out of control Mitch McMasters yelling and screaming in his best effort into intimidating Carter Franklin into doing something illegal. Normally he wasn't a fan of Carter, but today Raleigh was proud of him for finally having the backbone to make a tough decision and to stick with it. Raleigh let Carter tell the entire story. When he was finished, Raleigh spoke the sweetest words Carter Franklin had ever heard, "Son, you made the damn right decision. You will be just fine."

"Raleigh, are you sure, because have you reviewed their corporate documents lately?"

"Carter, I wrote every single one of those documents. You're damn right I am sure. Go have a beer and calm down. You are fine, son. If Mitch calls again, tell him to go piss up a rope."

Once their conversation was over, Raleigh began to laugh uncontrollably, because he knew that Mitch's bad day was about to get a lot worse. Raleigh was laughing so loud his secretaries could hear him in the lobby of the law office. If they had only known what had made their boss so happy, they would have joined in.

AROUND thirty minutes before Carter Franklin reached Raleigh J. Calhoun regarding Mitch McMaster's attempted loan advance, Raleigh had received some even more disturbing news for Mitch. Sheriff Buford Blakeley had delivered to Raleigh a search warrant requesting a DNA sample from Mitch McMasters. The summons stated that the sample was being requested in accordance with an investigation into the death of Haley Fulz. Buford asked Raleigh to have Mitch in his office by 3:30 pm; otherwise they would send some deputies to serve Mr. McMasters. Buford also informed Raleigh that he and Ernie would like to have an interview with Mr. McMasters once the DNA sample had been obtained. Raleigh stated that he would try to reach his client and have him available at the requested time. If there was a problem in reaching Mitch, he would immediately contact Buford.

Raleigh was getting ready to call Mitch when Carter Franklin called. Now, after hearing Franklin's story, he was relishing the chance to make Mitch's bad day get much, much worse. Upon contacting Mitch on his cell phone, Raleigh saved him any pleasantries and went straight to the heart of the matter, the court order for the DNA sample. "Mitch, this is Raleigh, you need to be in my office no later than 3:30 pm today."

After his meltdown with Carter Franklin and dealing with the fact that his million dollar line of credit had been wiped out, Mitch was in no mood to have Raleigh tell him what to do.

"Screw you, Raleigh! I'm busy."

"Ok, Mitch, Buford thought he would save you from the spectacle of having a couple of his deputies serve you in some public setting, but I will let him know you would prefer that method."

"What the hell are you talking about, Raleigh?"

"Never mind, Mitch, since you are too busy, you will find out when the deputies arrive."

Mitch was now really pissed off and scared to death. He immediately thought, "How in hell could this day get any worse." Then he found out the answer to his question.

"Dammit, Raleigh, what the hell are you talking about? What's this being served shit?"

"Mitch, I am in possession of a court ordered search warrant, signed by Judge Altus T. Claibourn, which commands a DNA sample from Mitch McMasters in accordance with an investigation into the death of Haley Fulz. Buford and Ernie will be here at 3:30 pm to obtain the sample and to ask you some questions. So Mitch, what shall I tell Sheriff Blakeley? Will you be here at the requested time or not?"

For a very brief moment, Mitch could not believe what he had just heard. His worst fears since the night of Haley's death were beginning to materialize. After spending thousands of dollars to keep people quiet, he was still facing the same daunting vision that had spurred him to try to cover up the entire matter. He was facing the prospect of having to answer questions being posed by Ernie Lambert and Buford Blakeley, not to mention a DNA sample. "Protest it, do something to make it go away. I don't care what you do, but just make it go away. Do you hear me, Raleigh?"

"Yea, I hear you alright, Mitch. It's really simple; either you voluntarily submit the sample, or they will put your ass in jail for contempt of court and will involuntarily obtain the sample. The choice is yours, Mitch. You can't intimidate your way out of a court ordered search warrant."

"You're no help. I can't do it. I just can't. You have to think of something and something quick." Raleigh could tell that Mitch was getting desperate. If Mitch wasn't such a jerk, Raleigh might have actually felt sorry for him. He could sense that the guy was about to break mentally and emotionally.

"Mitch, you have placed yourself in a position where there are no easy answers. Either you face the music in the setting of my office, or you will face it no telling where. If you really piss them off, they will serve you in the most embarrassing public setting they can find. It could be a Friday night football game, in a grocery store full of shoppers, or at a busy marina on the lake. I could file several motions objecting to the DNA search for various reasons, but we will lose, and it will expose you to public hearings on the matter. Public hearings, which I might add, that would more than likely be covered and reported on by your wife and your newspaper. You will look guilty simply by refusing to voluntarily furnish your DNA sample. It comes down to this; you have placed yourself in this position. So what's your decision, Mitch?"

Raleigh could hear Mitch's heavy breathing and trembling of his voice. The cocky, arrogant façade was long gone. What was left was a wounded and scared man, who was left with no friends and no place to turn. His money had run out and so had its perceived power. All that was left was a DNA test and the hope it would come back negative and that Ernie and Buford were simply on a fishing expedition. Mitch no longer held on to much hope for anything in his life. In a matter of ten days, he had gone from the most confident, powerful, and perceived wealthy man in the county to a pathetic, scared man, who was broke both financially and spiritually.

After a very long and uncomfortable silence Mitch McMasters informed Raleigh that he would be at his office at 3:30 pm. However, he was not discussing anything regarding Haley Fulz. "They can kiss my ass regarding Haley Fulz. It's just a damn fishing expedition, plain and simple. Just trying to make me look bad. If they ask about her, I will tell them to kiss my big fat ass. She was an employee and my son's girlfriend and that's that. I don't give a damn if you like it or not."

Raleigh took a deep breath and advised Mitch that he was within his legal rights not to answer their questions. But to do so would only add to a perception of guilt. Raleigh was tired of talking to his pathetic client. He closed the conversation with Mitch and promptly called Buford Blakely to inform him that they would see them at the appointed time.

THE meeting with Mitch McMasters, Ernie Lambert, and Buford Blakeley at the office of Raleigh J. Calhoun started promptly at 3:30 pm. The tension in the room was palpable. The only person in the room that wasn't nervous was Raleigh J. Calhoun. Mitch was scared to death and was unsuccessfully trying his best to conceal his desire to run out the front door, never to be seen again. Like the old Ozarkian saying for someone down on their luck, Mitch looked like death warmed over. Mitch presented himself with puffy bloodshot eyes, a very wrinkled orange sport shirt, messed up greasy hair, and his face looked as if he had aged thirty years during the past few days. If his appearance wasn't shocking enough, everyone present, except for Mitch, had the opportunity to catch the strong aroma of Budweiser beer coming from Mr. McMasters. It was evident that Mitch's drunken day at the lake had been interrupted by the hastily arranged meeting with Ernie and Buford.

Despite their experience in dealing with all types of criminal investigations, Ernie Lambert and Buford Blakeley were in unchartered territory in the interrogation of a person who had held so much sway and influence over Bouvier and all of Barry County. Clearly, it was intimidating to interrogate Mitch McMasters. Normally in these situations, Raleigh would try to lessen the tension in the room by offering coffee or soft drinks in order to bring about some initial conversation. Today Raleigh was relishing the sight of three of the most powerful men in the county sitting across from each other nervous as a bunch of whores in church. He immediately asked Ernie and Buford to state their business because they had called a meeting very abruptly and without the normal courtesies that he was accustomed. Raleigh was firm and direct in his communication with his old friends. Ernie and Buford were not alarmed, as they suspected Raleigh was posturing for his client.

The warrant issued by Judge Altus T. Claibourn was produced. Raleigh carefully examined it in the presence of the three. After he proclaimed it to be in order, Mitch abruptly grabbed it, "I want to see the damn thing." Mitch read it twice, primarily to annoy the other three. "So you got Altus to go along with your boneheaded detective work. He's such a chicken shit. You know, he really is. I guess he's going to go down with the two of you. When your little investigation blows up in your faces, I will be parading your failure all over the front page of the *Gazette*."

Ernie glanced over to a clearly perturbed Buford Blakeley and nodded his head as is to say, "Hang in there, we expected this from the chicken shit of all chicken shits."

The DNA swab of Mitch McMasters was conducted without further incident. After that was completed, Buford began with the first of what he and Ernie had planned to be a lengthy list of questions for the esteemed Mr. McMasters. The questioning immediately hit a brick wall. Mitch's answer to the first question was, "I am not answering any of your damn questions. And if you don't like it, then either kiss my ass or arrest me."

After everyone in the room got over the surprise of Mitch's angry response, Buford tried again. Question number two received the same response. A very perturbed and red faced Buford Blakeley tried a third time to elicit a response from the arrogant and beer laden suspect, but the result from Mitch was the same.

Sensing that he was really getting under Buford's skin, Mitch shot back in a very cocky manner, "What's your next question, Buford?"

It was evident to Raleigh that his client was like a proud and arrogant wounded animal that had been backed into a corner. Mitch was desperate and was lashing out in his final attempt to save himself. The effects of the alcohol were certainly not helping matters either. As was the case of the night Haley died, Mitch McMasters' anger would come boiling from the surface when faced with stressful situations while under the influence of alcohol. To put it bluntly, he was a mean and unreasonable drunk.

Buford walked over to Mitch and got as close as he could get to Mitch without actually touching him. The intrusion of his personal sphere clearly annoyed Mitch.

"Dammit, Buford, get the hell away from me."

Raleigh spoke up as well, "Buford, let's just let things calm down for a moment. Have a seat and things will go much better."

As much as he liked and respected Raleigh, Buford wasn't budging. With his nose within an inch of Mitch's Buford whispered to Mitch, "We know you killed Haley. The thing we don't know for sure if it was an accident when you ran her off the road, or did you intentionally run the convertible, you know, the one you bought for her, off the road to kill her?"

Mitch sat in his chair, with his eyes squinted, as his body shook from anger and probably fear. No one had ever had the guts to challenge him face to face in the manner like Sheriff Buford Blakeley had at that moment. He looked like an animal ready to strike and attack its enemy.

Just before he started to walk back to his seat, Buford glanced over to Mitch and said, "Did you really screw her one last time right before you killed her?"

That question was not part of Ernie's plan and rightfully so. Because once it was uttered, Mitch McMasters became unglued. He dove across the table and tried to grab Buford by the throat. Raleigh J. Calhoun's elegant conference room became a whirl of commotion as his secretary came rushing in to see what was the matter. She opened the door only to see Raleigh and Ernie trying to pull apart Buford and Mitch.

Mitch was yelling, "Go screw yourself, you perverted bastard. Go to hell, Buford, and take your little buddy, Erniepoo, with you. Screw the both of you."

Raleigh and Ernie finally got their respective parties separated and began to pick up the various documents that had gone flying all over the conference room as the fight broke out. Before Ernie and Buford left Raleigh's office, Buford looked over at Mitch and said, "Considering your response, Mitch, she must have been as good as the rumors we've heard."

Mitch began to yell all types of vulgarities at Buford. As Buford was being pushed out the door by Ernie, he yelled back, "Good to see you, Mitch. The next time we will have the handcuffs ready for your guilty ass."

As they headed out of Raleigh's office, a delighted Buford Blakeley glanced over at Ernie Lambert and said, "I thought that went pretty well."

Ernie disgustedly replied, "No, Buford, it did not go well at all."

"Well, I sure had a good time. He's such a guilty weasel. He's never had anyone really back him in a corner before. Man, was it fun."

Ernie Lambert just shook his head. Deep down he enjoyed seeing Mitch lose it as much as Buford did, but he knew he couldn't express that to Buford because it would be like turning a kid loose with a water hose. Any moral support could embolden Buford, and he could envision every future Buford Blakeley interrogation being a real donnybrook. As much as this one situation was fun, there simply was no place for it in real crime investigations.

As they walked back to his office, Ernie bucked up Buford by relating to him that once they got Willie's part of the broader investigation on the record, namely getting Alex

Vander discussing the meth operation on tape, they would then indict Mitch McMasters for Haley's death. If things went as planned, within the next week Buford would get the honor of placing handcuffs on Mitch McMasters and reading him his Miranda rights.

Before he left Raleigh J. Calhoun's office, Mitch calmed down enough to sit down with Raleigh. Raleigh proceeded to explain all of the things that Mitch shouldn't have done in the meeting.

"Mitch, you looked desperate, stupid, and guilty today."

The remark did not sit well with an already agitated Mitch McMasters. "Thanks a lot, Raleigh. I didn't see you throwing any great legal wisdom into the mix. I pretty much felt like I was all on my own in that meeting. The way I see it, it's just a fishing expedition on their part. A good attorney would have stopped the damn thing before it even started. But like I said, I didn't see you coming up with any creative legal strategies to counter Ernie Lambert and that dufus Buford Blakeley. God, it looks like you could out maneuver those two."

Raleigh took his verbal condemnation from Mitch McMasters very calmly and didn't appear to be a bit agitated. He grinned and looked down at Mitch, with his reading glasses perched on the end of his nose, "Well, Mitch, I am glad you understand the legal basis for search warrants so well. Your understanding of the law will serve you well when you are representing yourself in the second degree murder case that the State of Missouri is getting ready to bring against you."

"Screw you, Raleigh. No case is going to be brought against Mitch McMasters."

"Sorry to burst your ill-informed bubble, Mitch, but you are about to be indicted for the murder of Haley Fulz. Right before the start of our meeting, I asked Ernie if he really had a case or if he was still fishing. Guess what, Mitch; Ernie looked me straight in the eye and said, 'We have the bastard. The case is practically over.' So you need to be thinking about whether you want a new attorney. By the way, do you want to try to plea bargain this thing down to a lesser charge?"

"There is nothing to think over. Ernie is just jerking your chain, and you are so gullible you actually believe his jive."

"Mitch, I have known Ernie Lambert for a long time. He has never lied to me or tried to blow smoke up my ass regarding the strength of his case. If he doesn't have a case, he will tell you. And if he has a tight case, he will tell you how bad your client's position is. So Mitch, from what I have gathered today, you are in some really deep shit. Have a great evening, and I strongly suggest that you seriously consider the two items I just mentioned."

Mitch McMasters had heard enough bad news for one day, and he was tired of fighting. Without saying a word, he simply walked out of Raleigh J. Calhoun's office and drove back to his lake house. He spent the rest of the evening meandering up and down the lake, drinking beer, contemplating his legal fate, and how he could escape the impending indictment. Other than the night Haley Fulz died, it had to have been the worst night of Mitch McMasters life. As the night wore on, a spiritual awakening came upon him as he began to see the simplicity of his actions. He kept asking himself, 'Why couldn't I have been happy with my life? Why couldn't I have been more understanding and gracious toward other's feelings and desires? Why was I so self absorbed and so full of arrogance and pride that I would risk everything for not only a seventeen year old girl, but my very own son's beloved girlfriend? I have ruined my life because of my arrogance, my pride, and my desire for instant self gratification. So many times I made fun and belittled the guys who did the right things. You know, the guys who were faithful to their wives and were always there for their kids. How could I have been so stupid? How could I have been so wrong? Right now, I would give anything to be one of those people.'

The last thing Mitch McMasters did before he passed out on his boat was to dial the phone number of a man that he had belittled and ridiculed over the years, the Reverend Durwood Hardy. He didn't speak with Reverend Hardy, but at 3:17 am a very intoxicated Mitch McMasters left the following messag; on the Durwood Hardy's voice mail, "Durwood, this is Mitch McMasters. I'm sorry to bother you at this time of the night. But I need you to pray for me. Please, please pray for me. Please! I need your help and understanding more than you will ever know. Good night."

CHAPTER 20

AS the sun began to rise at Roaring River State Park, two early bird anglers were awakened to the ghastly sight of a man hanging from Deer Leap Cliff, which was a two hundred foot scenic overlook in the main fishing channel of the park. The man appeared to be dead as there was no motion coming from his body. A large tow rope was wrapped around his neck with the other end of the rope tied to a large boulder. The shocked men quickly got the attention of a park ranger who soon realized that the man hanging lifeless over Roaring River State Park was Willie Stillwagon.

Sheriff Buford Blakeley was quickly dispatched to the scene. Buford was assisted by the coroner and park ranger's staff in the retrieval of Willie's body from the scenic cliff, which up until this moment, had been one of Buford's favorite places in the park. From that moment forward the Deer Leap Cliff would forever be a horribly painful reminder of where his old friend lost his tormented life. Even though Willie had committed himself to some terrible life choices and had broken a trust that Buford had placed in him, Buford still had a soft spot for Willie and would for the rest of his life. When they finally got possession of Willie's body, Buford sat on the cliff and cried uncontrollably. He had so many questions, questions that he knew would more than likely never be answered. The question that gnawed at him the most was, 'Who would be next?'

Even though the coroner hadn't had enough time to make a determination of the cause of death, Buford was confident in his appraisal that this was a murder, not a suicide. There were so many other ways to kill oneself, and Willie wasn't the type who would want to go out in such an overly public way. Buford quickly surmised that whoever killed Willie wanted everyone to take notice of the act. And what would be a better way to get everyone's attention than to hang him off the highest and most visible point in the park.

By the time Ernie Lambert reached the scene, questions were racing in both Ernie's and Buford's minds. The first was how did this happen when Willie was supposed to be under the surveillance of two federal marshals. Secondly, where was Brad Ellsworth? Was he safe or were they about to make another gruesome discovery? Third, was Brad's friend, Brandon Farve, the real Brandon alive and well?

Ernie Lambert assembled the federal agents and Buford Blakeley in his office where they convened via conference call with the head of the Missouri State Police. The feds reluctantly admitted that they lost contact with Willie shortly before midnight. They had no clue as to what happened to him. They initially assumed that he had made contact with Alex Vander, per their plan, and would lure Alex to their standard meeting spot, which was wired with all types of surveillance devices. They set up their detail near the assigned meeting spot, but Willie and Vander never materialized. The agents were able to make phone contact with Brad Ellsworth. He was at work in the park and had heard about Willie's death. He was terribly distraught. Brad informed the agents that he had been in contact with his friend, Brandon Farve, and he was safe. Now that Willie was dead, Ernie knew it was of the utmost importance to get both Brad and Brandon under protection.

Additionally, Brandon's testimony would bring added weight since he was Willie's primary mule and the one who took the toughest assignments.

The next order of business was the issuance of an arrest warrant for special agent Alex Vander. They had initially wanted to get the case against Vander locked up as tight as possible before moving in with an arrest, but Willie's horrible death had changed things and changed them quickly. When Ernie made this decision, there were all sorts of yelling and screaming going on between the head of the state police and feds. Each had a compelling reason why they should or should not advance and advance quickly toward Vander. Ernie eventually won with the presentation that Vander apparently had access to a substantial amount of cash, which would assist him in a quick get away. Additionally, he knew there was no way they could keep the integrity of the investigation under wraps after Willie's death. Vander needed to be apprehended as soon as possible. Mercifully for Mitch McMasters, Willie Stillwagon's gruesome death moved the indictment of Mitch for Haley Fulz death to the side, at least for a few days.

THE arrest of Alex Vander did not turn out to be as smooth as Ernie Lambert and Buford Blakeley had planned. Agents patrolling Vander's home and his usual haunts turned up no signs of Vander. He was supposed to report to work at 4:00 pm the afternoon following Willie's death, but he didn't show, nor did he call in with an excuse. This had never happened in all the years Vander worked for the Barry County Sheriff's department or the Missouri State Police. When he failed to report to work, Lambert sensed that Vander had killed Willie after being tipped off that Willie had turned on him. He suspected that Vander had fled with his and Willie's money.

The nearest airports in Springfield, Missouri; Bentonville, Arkansas; Tulsa, Oklahoma; Kansas City, Missouri; and St. Louis, Missouri were on alert with photos and detailed descriptions of Alex Vander.

IN the midst of the commotion surrounding the whereabouts of Alex Vander, Buford Blakeley received a surprising call from a Missouri Water Patrol agent, who worked the Castle Rock area of the lake. The agent reported that a boat registered to Mitch McMasters had been found by some fishermen earlier in the day. When the fishermen discovered the boat, it was unoccupied and floating aimlessly with the current of the lake. The agent reported that he had contacted Mrs. McMasters who was on her way to meet with the agent. Buford agreed to meet with them once he could shake free from the investigation of Vander.

Blakeley rounded up Ernie Lambert, and they hurriedly made their way to the McMasters' lake cabin. When they arrived, they found the Water Patrol agent, Clare McMasters, Veronica Hardy, and the Reverend Durwood Hardy. Blakeley and Lambert were caught off guard by the presence of Durwood and Veronica, but they soon discovered their connection.

Clare McMasters was clearly distraught. She began to explain that she had received a call from Durwood Hardy recounting a message that Mitch McMasters had apparently left sometime in the night on Hardy's phone. After several unsuccessful tries to reach McMasters, Hardy contacted Clare. Clare stated that she immediately came to the lake house and found nothing, except for Mitch's cell phone, which showed a call to Durwood Hardy at 3:17 am. She informed everyone that she found the house, just as it was at the moment, with two chairs overturned. Just as she was about to call Blakeley to report Mitch's disappearance, she stated she received the call from the Water Patrol agent reporting Mitch's boat drifting unoccupied in the main channel of the lake. Clare explained that she and Mitch had grown apart in the past few months. However, the estrangement had become more pronounced since Haley's death. They had barely been communicating over the past couple of weeks.

"He could have been gone for a week before I would have known it. He had become almost like a recluse, just wanting to stay on the lake and drink. Tell me, please, what do you know about Mitch? I need to know what is going on, because all day I have heard the whispers that Willie's death was tied to meth and Alex Vander. And then right before I left to come down here, a source informed me Willie also had a connection with Haley's death and that pertained to Mitch. So guys, please tell me what the hell is going on?"

Before he would answer, Ernie Lambert asked the Water Patrol agent to leave the room. Clare insisted upon the Hardys remaining with her.

"Clare, I cannot discuss anything with you at this time. We have an investigation that is at a critical and very delicate point. Events with regard to the investigation are happening so fast I cannot really grasp their magnitude."

Clare wasn't pleased with Ernie's answer. She was angry for so many reasons. "So can you confirm or deny whether Willie was a key witness in the investigation into Haley's death and that Mitch is the prime suspect?"

"I will tell you this, Clare; Mitch is the key suspect in Haley's death, and he damn well knows it."

Clare broke down and began to cry. Ernie Lambert had just confirmed the deepest fear she had possessed since Haley's death. "So he was the father of her unborn child. Oh my God! How could this have happened? I trusted and loved Haley. I know Mitch has his demons, but to screw around with your very own son's teenage girlfriend is beyond imagination. Am I right or not?"

"Clare, I cannot verify that claim."

"Do you think there is a tie to Willie's death and Mitch's disappearance? From what I hear, you are about to indict him for murder, with Willie as your prime witness?"

"Clare, Willie's death and Mitch's disappearance may or may not be related. But I can assure you, finding Mitch is a top priority for us."

The Water Patrol agent reentered the cabin and confirmed that Mitch was seen by a couple of fishermen docking his boat around 4:00 am. However, when the manager of the marina arrived to start his work day at 5:30 am Mitch's boat was gone from the dock. Apparently he placed the phone call to Durwood Hardy while on the water at 3:17 am, docked the boat around 4:00 am, and left once again before 5:30 am. This time he left his lake cabin without his cell phone. To Clare McMasters, this was the most perplexing tidbit of information because she knew Mitch never went anywhere without his cell phone, unless he was going somewhere against his will.

As they were about to conclude their meeting, Clare pointed her finger at Ernie and Buford, "You better move fast before anyone else ends up dead. I think Willie and Mitch have been murdered as a result of whatever investigation you have going. I hope and pray I am wrong. I also hope and pray you get this mess under control before no telling how many others end up dying."

Once they were out of earshot of Clare McMasters, Ernie Lambert angrily told Buford Blakeley, "Round up Brandon one and Brandon two, Brad and Brandon, whatever the hell their names are. You know what I mean. Round them up

ASAP! We have to get them into a safe setting. I'm afraid they could be next. Willie's death, suicide, murder, or whatever it was, would have taken place during Brad's shift at the park. As sneaky as he is and as close as he was with Willie, I cannot believe he didn't see something. Let me know when you have more information on the manhunt for Alex Vander."

Blakeley hustled off to his command post. As he drove away, Lambert wondered how much worse the investigation could go. Had he gone from being on the verge of a legendary criminal indictment to an embarrassingly blown investigation in a matter of twenty-four hours? Only time would tell, and he hated having his fate tied up in the hands of a sneaky kid who went by the names of Brandon and Brad.

AFTER the third day, Lambert and Blakeley whispered to each other, but definitely not to anyone else, that they believed Vander was long gone with the cash and would never be seen again. Vander and McMasters' disappearances had become the talk of the town. The scores of misguided stories and gossip were flying rampant around town. Everyone had their own theory as to what had happened to Willie, Alex Vander, and Mitch McMasters. The scary thing to Lambert and Blakeley was that most of the citizens of Bouvier knew just as much as they did regarding what had happened.

Three strange things happened in the week following the disappearances of Vander and McMasters. The first was the notification from the Destin, Florida, prosecutor's office that they were in the possession of a hot check in the amount of $125,478 payable to Pate Johnston. The hot check was drawn on the bank account of Mitch McMasters. Apparently, Johnston had deposited the check from McMasters and then immediately started writing checks all over Destin. The largest check was for the purchase of a boat. Once the bank in Destin was notified that the check from McMasters was hot, all of the checks written by Johnston were returned as well. This had caused a big mess for Johnston and for several Destin businessmen. As expected, the prosecutor in Destin was hot and had placed an arrest warrant for Mitch McMasters for felony check writing charges, along other lesser crimes. He informed Buford Blakeley that he wanted McMasters arrested immediately.

Blakeley laughed and replied, "Well, you are going to have to stand in line with the rest of us poor bastards."

The prosecutor failed to find the humor in Blakeley's reply, nor was he laughing when Blakeley explained the rest of the story behind McMasters' disappearance.

Blakeley concluded the call by saying, "If you find him, send him our way."

Blakeley contacted Johnston, who vaguely explained what his daughter had witnessed with Mitch and Haley. Johnston told Buford how Mitch had "forced" them to move to Florida, only to be given fraudulent checks upon their arrival in Destin. He could barely contain his laughter when he heard Johnston's story. He thought, 'There couldn't be two guys who deserve each other more than Pate Johnston and Mitch McMasters.'

The second interesting event was the receipt of the DNA test, which determined that Mitch McMasters wasn't the father of Haley Fulz unborn baby. Mitch McMasters was not the father of the baby. This gave more credence to Brad Ellsworth's story that he had been sexually involved with Haley prior to Mitch coming into the picture. The DNA test results, combined with the hush money paid to Pate Johnston, caused Ernie to contemplate the irony of Mitch's situation,

'He did everything in his power to cover up his actions when, in fact, he wasn't even the father of Haley's child.'

THE third event was the most startling. A Fed Ex priority mail package arrived at Buford Blakeley's home. As soon as he opened the package, Buford knew it was not your ordinary Fed Ex delivery. Enclosed were two typed messages and a tightly wrapped large manila envelope.

The first message read:

We are safe. But we wouldn't have been if we hadn't taken matters into our own hands. After AV killed Willie, no one was going to be safe. All of us, you included, were going to be the next to hang off Deer Leap. On the night of Willie's hanging, AV and Willie were going to their regular meeting spot and then AV suddenly turned around. We followed as best as we could, without being noticed. But we were too late to save Willie. We saw the bastard throw Willie off the cliff. It was the most horrible sight. You can't imagine how horrible. With Willie dead, we knew the investigations of AV and Mitch McMasters would be dead as well. Everyone would be scared to death to step forward. You will find AV and Mitch soon. Scum eventually rises to the surface.

The other envelope is a little thank you from us for doing the right thing. Trying to bring down AV and Mitch McMasters was the right thing to do. Willie's money is safe, as well. Willie had more money than we could ever think about spending. Combine that with AV's stash and you can only imagine what we are managing at the moment. Will split it with you when the time is right. You are a good man and the other package is a down payment for your good work and intentions. If you ever get down to Key West look us up. We bought a boat in Willie's honor. We named it, "Willie's Loot." The second letter

*can be used for your investigation files. Please destroy this
letter after reading.*
  Take care,
  Brad and Brandon.

The second letter was a more sanitized version of the first.
It conveniently left out their admission to being involved in
the disappearances of Alex Vander and Mitch McMasters
and especially any reference to having Willie and Alex
Vander's drug money. The second letter clearly spelled out the
eyewitness account of the murder of Willie Stillwagon by Alex
Vander and gave no indication as to Vander's whereabouts. It
was signed Brad Ellsworth and Brandon Farve.

After reading both letters, Buford's hands were shaking as he
started to carefully open the large manila envelope. The green
color of the $100 dollar bills immediately got his attention, as
did the impressive quantity. Buford's first guess was that the
envelope contained at least $10,000. But he was way off. To
be more accurate, his estimate was only ten percent correct.
When he completed counting, the stash totaled $100,000. He
immediately locked it in his fire proof firearms vault located
in the basement of his home. Buford promised himself to play
it smart and to never flaunt his windfall. He might need the
cash if the botched investigations of Alex Vander and Mitch
McMasters ended up getting him beat in the next Sheriff's
election. It was nice knowing he had a secret stash of cash in
case times got tough.

CHAPTER 21

SIX weeks after Alex Vander's disappearance, a group of fishermen made the startling and ghastly discovery of a man floating on the surface of the lake near Castle Rock. The dead man tied to a wooden rocking chair was Alex Vander. Apparently Vander had been strapped down to the chair, which had been anchored by concrete blocks. By the visible signs of struggle, he was alive when initially tossed into the lake water. It took six weeks for the rope to break loose from the concrete block. Two days later, another group of fishermen made s similar discovery. Only this time it was the body of Mitch McMasters. The rocking chairs used to tie down the bodies of Vander and McMasters were the same chairs that Clare McMasters had noticed missing from the porch of their lake cabin. Ironically, they were the same chairs Mitch McMasters and Haley Fulz were seen happily and romantically occupying just two months earlier.

THE Bouvier volleyball team was playing for the district championship the day Mitch McMasters' body was recovered. The team had dedicated their season in honor of Haley and was on the verge of their first championship. Each team member had Haley's number seven sewn on the upper right corner of their uniform. It had been too painful for Haley's mom to attend most games, but tonight she was determined to be in attendance for the district championship game. She knew how much Haley had desired a championship in her senior year of high school. Before she left for the game, Jackie Fulz reached into the bag that Haley used for her volleyball uniform. She wanted to touch Haley's uniform, maybe for good luck and maybe just to feel like she was still in contact with her beloved daughter in some way.

In the bag she felt a piece of paper below Haley's uniform. Jackie pulled out the paper and discovered it be a short note written to Mitch from Haley. Mitch had replied back on the same piece of paper. As she read it, Jackie began to cry. However, they were bittersweet tears. From the letter she could tell it was written by two people deeply in love. The letter answered the lingering question that had plagued Jackie Fulz since Haley's death. What had brought Mitch and Haley together? Now she knew. They were both lonely romantics who had fallen head over heels for each other.

Before she left her home for the game, Jackie Fulz did as she did every night. She said a short prayer for Haley's soul and memory. That night Jackie Fulz spent her first night truly at peace since Haley's death, beaming as she watched the Bouvier girls hoist the championship trophy in honor of their beloved number seven, Haley Fulz.

Now that Mitch McMasters and Alex Vander had been found, Buford Blakeley announced to his staff that he was doing something he had not done in more than ten years. He was taking a much deserved vacation. A stunned staff inquired into his destination. A smiling Sheriff Blakeley replied, "Key West, going to visit some family and tend to some family business."

One of the staff members yelled out, "Don't forget to come back."

Buford smiled and thought to himself, "If Willie and A.V. had as much money as I think they did, I may never come back."

CPSIA information can be obtained at www.ICGtesting.com
Printed in the USA
LVOW060900280413

331232LV00001B/3/P